Shelter in Garnet Run

ROAN PARRISH

Originally distributed via Patron for The Happily Ever After Collective, April, 2023

Published December, 2023

ISBN: 9781949749175

Original cover design by Timmi Meskers

Content Warnings

Below is a list of things that might be difficult for some readers to encounter. Take care of yourself <3

- mention of drugs
- mention of addiction
- mention of parental abuse
- taxidermy/animal death (not pets!)
- mention of transphobia
- discussion of dysphoria
- descriptions of physical unwellness

CHAPTER 1

River

Ten minutes before closing, headlights swept through the trees as a truck rounded the driveway and came to a stop in the parking lot of the Dirt Road Cat Shelter. People always did this—thought that as long as they dashed through the door before it was locked then they could take their sweet time playing with the cats.

Usually, River Mills didn't mind. The chance of a cat getting adopted was well worth the loss of personal time. Not like they were really doing much after closing other than playing with the cats, anyway.

Tonight, though, they were exhausted. All they wanted to do was take a hot shower, smoke some weed, and have popcorn for dinner while they watched the final three episodes of *Surprise, You're Married*. They were pretty sure three of the couples didn't have a chance in hell of making it.

The doors flew open in a gust of cold wind, pine needles, and exhaust. A large, broad man who appeared to be wrapped in a blanket rushed toward them.

"I'm so glad you're still open," the man said from inside his thick scarf. "I wasn't sure where else to go."

River glanced up into concerned brown eyes. The man uncovered a bundle in his arms. The blanket wasn't wrapped around him; it was wrapped around a small, trembling cat.

"I found it on the side of the road. I thought it was dead, but when I went to pick it up ..."

The cat looked bad. Nearly frozen and undernourished, it probably would've died in the night if he hadn't found it. River's heart began to pound and a familiar tightness banded their chest.

"Bring it in here."

The man followed them without question as they found a box to keep the cat warm and turned on a heating pad. He placed the bundle in the box gently, stroking the cat's ear with a fingertip before withdrawing.

River put the box on the heating pad and tucked the blanket around the cat. Better to warm it up first before checking for any other injuries or illnesses. The cat could sleep next to their bed so they could get up every couple hours and give it formula if it was strong enough to eat. Then they'd call Molly tomorrow morning and see if she could come take a look at the poor little thing.

River just hoped it would last that long. Nausea bubbled up in their gut. The last time someone had brought in a cat, it hadn't made it. Too young, too weak, it had died in their arms three hours later.

"... Darling."

River tuned back in and the man's hand was extended.

"What? Sorry."

"I'm Cassidy Darling."

Did you honestly think for one second that this dude was calling you *"darling"?*

They shook hands. The man's palm was rough and dry, his fingers long.

There were people who introduced themselves with their full names, right off the bat. From most people, it seemed self-aggrandizing, as if their reputation preceded them. But from Cassidy

Darling it struck River as anachronistic instead. A throwback to a time when a full name had the power to conjure an entire story.

"River."

They walked back out to the front desk, hoping he would get the hint and take off. But he stopped at the desk with them.

"Do you think it's gonna be okay, River?"

His voice caressed their name and their scalp prickled pleasantly.

"Global climate change, inflation, the denial of bodily autonomy, and the rise of fascism suggest no," they muttered.

Excitement sparked in the man's eyes and he unwound his scarf, opened his wool overcoat, and began to unbutton his gray flannel shirt.

"Uhh."

River froze, squinted their eyes half-shut, and held up their hand, as if they could ward off whatever was about to happen.

Their boss had definitely failed to address what to do if a patron strips in front of you in the employee handbook. Well. Less *handbook* and more pieces of paper covered in Rye's cramped handwriting and River's revisions held together with a paper clip in the bottom drawer.

Cassidy spread open his muted winter layers to reveal a bright yellow T-shirt that said *Tell Me About It*. He made a Vanna White gesture at the shirt.

"Um. Is that ...*Jokerman?*"

"The font? I don't know. My sister made it for me. I'll ask her."

He was typing on his phone before River could say anything.

Ohh, he was agreeing with me. Via shirt.

"Her answer was a grin emoji. Does that mean it is?"

"I know it is. Never mind. I don't know about the cat, but I'll have the vet come take a look tomorrow."

"She says 'that's the joke.' What the hell does that mean?"

Before, River had seen only a flip book of moods—worried, excited, confused. But when Cassidy looked up from his phone, River took in his features for the first time.

He had warm brown eyes and a short, full beard. When he smiled, it revealed a space between his two front teeth and smile lines around his eyes. A thin, gold ring gleamed in his nose and his brown hair was in a parted quiff with the sides faded.

Wow.

Cassidy buttoned his shirt up to the neck again, obliterating the color with gray flannel, the flannel with wool. He wound the black scarf around his neck again.

"I'll get out of your hair," he said. "You're probably eager to get home."

He pulled leather gloves from his coat pocket and turned to leave. Then he turned back to River.

"Is there any chance, if I left my phone number, that you could let me know if the cat is okay? I'll just worry is all."

"Are you sure?" they asked. "I mean, do you want to know if it's not okay too."

He nodded and River believed him.

"Okay, then."

"Should I write it down for whoever's working tomorrow?"

"It's me. I'm working tomorrow."

And the day after that and the day after that.

Cassidy smiled warmly.

"Well I guess I should give you my number, then."

Is this guy flirting with me?

They created a new contact in their phone, then handed it to Cassidy.

"Is Jokerman a *bad* thing, though?" he asked, handing back River's phone.

"Yes. It's hideous. Like, famously maligned."

"Hmm. Is a jokerman like a merman?" Cassidy asked.

"I never thought of it like that."

Visions of creatures that were half human and half playing card danced in River's head.

"I've got some googling to do," Cassidy said. "Good night, River. Thanks for your help."

Then he smiled at them and their stomach had the absolute gall to fill with butterflies.

"Mhm, night," River managed as blood rushed in their ears.

Cassidy swept through the front doors of the Dirt Road Cat Shelter like an angel of death in his long black coat. And River went to check on the cat whose life he might have just saved.

CHAPTER 2

River

"Thank you so much for coming," River's brother Adam said, hugging them. He glanced over his shoulder to make sure they weren't overheard. When he saw the coast was clear, he hissed, "She knows everything."

She referred to Gus, River's nine-year-old niece, and *everything*, in this instance, referred to Christmas presents.

DEAR GOD HELP, read the text River had gotten from Adam the previous afternoon. *She says she knows what her xmas presents are bc of the cookies on the computer? Gotta go old school— can you come early??*

Then a string of emojis that made it clear their brother was at his wit's end.

River adored Gus, but in moments like these they were deeply grateful not to be her parent.

"Hey, River."

Wes, Adam's partner, put a hand on their shoulder for a brief pat. Then he, too, glanced around for Gus and lowered his voice.

"She knows. Every month she gets smarter. Where is it gonna end?"

The horror on his face was genuine, amusing coming from

someone who had three snakes, a tarantula, two raccoons, a number of lizards and leeches, and was basically a genius.

"She probably plotting your death right now," River said, then winked at Gus, who'd come in while they were talking. "Oh my god, she's right behind you!"

Gus dove at Wes and Adam's legs as Wes turned, arms in a defensive position. Adam shrieked and went down like a sacked quarterback. Or whoever gets sacked in football. Point was, he crumpled.

Gus, always one to seize the moment, climbed on top of him and pinned his arms.

"Hi, Daddy," she said, and dropped a kiss on the tip of his nose. "What're you doing on the floor?"

She scrambled off him and tugged on Wes' arm.

"Aren't you going to help him?"

Wes bent and hauled Adam upright, pulling him close to his side and kissing his head.

"You okay?"

"Yeah," Adam grumbled. "At least this time I got bullied *before* going to the mall instead of at it."

He straightened his clothes and squared his shoulders.

"Gus," he said seriously. "You can't dive bomb people. It's dangerous. People could hit their heads or break a hip or ..."

"Daddy, I didn't dive bomb you. I just kinda startled you and bumped your legs and you fell over."

Adam flushed.

"Well, then, it's dangerous to semi-dive bomb people because some of us have hyper-reactive nervous systems. Okay?"

"Got it." She twirled a piece of hair around her finger absently and cocked her head. "Why do you have a hyperactive nervous system?"

"All righty," Wes said, grabbing her and swinging her upside down in a way that always made her squeal with delight as she squirmed like a fish on the line. "We're going to the mall. This is a sign of how much we adore you because there is no place on earth more unpleasant than the mall in the month before the holidays."

"Or any time," Adam mumbled.

"Why's it called a mall?" Gus asked.

"I'm gonna let you and River google that one after we're gone," Adam said. He bent and kissed the top of her messy head. "Can't wait to hear about the etymology when we get home."

Neon, the cat Adam had adopted for Gus last Christmas stalked into the room, all sass and fluff. Adam scooped her up and kissed her orange head. She meowed and licked his hair. Although the cat had been intended for Gus, she was much more interested in her lizard, and since Wes had many pets of his own, Neon became Adam's by default. Though River was pretty sure Adam liked it that way.

"Oh, do you want to come to the movies with us on Saturday?" Adam asked. "We're taking Gus to see the animated *Rudolph the Red-Nosed Reindeer* for the first time."

"Yes, come!" Gus said, looping her arm through theirs.

"Wish I could, Bug, but it's Craftmas this weekend and Rye and I got a booth for the shelter."

"Right, I forgot that was this weekend," Adam said. "Maybe we should come visit you."

"What's Craftmas?" Wes asked.

"It's like a farmer's market, but for Christmassy crafts, food, gifts, and stuff," Adam said. "I used to go with my mom as a little kid."

"*You're* going to Craftmas?" Gus asked River. She looked horrified.

"Yeah. What?"

"Um, you hate talking to people, you hate being looked at, you hate Christmas," she said, ticking the reasons off on her fingers. "And you *really* hate when large groups of people are excited together."

"What? No I don't!"

The fingers came out again. "When we watched that football game and everyone cheered, you were like, 'Sheep'"

River couldn't argue with her on that one.

"You left trick-or-treating early because you said it was too many people being excited all at once."

"I said it was too many people who might *puke* being excited too close to *me*," they clarified.

"And last Valentine's Day when I asked you what kind of cards I should make for my class, you told me that Valentine's Day capitalizes on the patriarchal dread of woman who might choose to be alone to make people exchange recyclables and hydrogenated vegetable oil."

River really couldn't argue with that either.

"Fine, but I don't *hate* Christmas."

Gus shrugged a world-weary, silent film shrug—a shrug far too old for her nine years—and said, "I guess we'll see."

Adam gawked at Gus. "Your memory terrifies me."

Gus grinned.

CHAPTER 3

River

River: *Oingo Boingo and Tillie will be good to bring, I think. They'll stay pretty calm even if kids poke at them.*

Rye: *And we have to bring the kittens, right? Ppl shit themselves for kittens*

River: *Well by all means let's make them shit themselves.*

River: *I think Boo should come too. And Peach Melba won't let him out of her sight so she'll invite herself.*

Rye: *Yeah, make* sure *they get adopted together.*

River: *Def. And then we can plan day two based on who gets adopted tomorrow.*

Rye: *Yup. See you there. I'll bring coffee.*

River: *I'll bring my own coffee, thanks though!*

Rye: *Dude, why does everyone hate my coffee?? There's nothing wrong with it!*

River: *No comment.*

River: *My babieeees :(*

Rye: *I know :(*

River didn't hate Christmas.

Christmas songs were awful. Red and green looked straight-up hideous together. Eggnog was revolting. But that didn't mean they *hated* Christmas.

They just didn't like it very much.

The people who attended Craftmas? Yeah, they *loved* Christmas. And every year they descended upon the Whitstable Convention Center, ten miles west of Garnet Run, with enough cheer to light up a Christmas tree.

They came from far and wide, so this year, as the only no-kill shelter in a fifty-mile radius, Rye and River had decided to staff an adoption booth, hoping to place a large number of the shelter's cats in loving homes.

It was only this that had—or could have—convinced River to vend at Craftmas.

Yeah, Gus had been irritatingly right about that too. They did hate talking to strangers. They did hate being looked at. And both at the same time while also navigating whatever bananas shit was almost guaranteed to happen around Christmas superfans? A fucking nightmare.

A long, high *mew* from the seat next to them announced the parking lot, already half full even though the doors didn't open for three hours.

"That's right," they told the cats, stroking Tillie's soft orange fur through a small opening in her cat carrier. "I wouldn't do this for anyone but you. So just look cute, be sweet, and don't do anything weird."

Rye's head and torso were sticking out a propped open door and he gestured River over as soon as they drove in.

"Hurry, hurry."

"Is this where we load in?"

"Not officially, but our table is right through here and the official entrance is way the hell over there."

He was already pulling open the van door. What it would be like to have the confidence to flout rules the way Rye did?

They cooed at the cats as they carried Millie and Oingo inside. When they'd emptied the van inside the doors, they tossed River the keys and hurried inside to see to the cats.

The huge room was bursting at the seams with the sights, smells, sounds, and emotional lability of the holidays. Tables and booths were arranged into five aisles, Christmas music piped from speakers all around, overloud and echoey in the mostly empty space. A huge Christmas tree, hung with tinsel, fairy lights, and elaborate glass ornaments sat on a platform in the center of the room, looming high above the crowd like an evergreen panopticon.

The Dirt Road Cat Shelter's table was draped with a green tablecloth, and a folded card that said RESERVED rested on top. The table next to theirs sported a red tablecloth. On each, a single candy cane sat in front of the card.

"Here we are," they told the cats.

River kept up a steady stream of chatter to keep them calm during set-up. Once the cages were WD-40ed, the short leg of the table was shimmed with a folded-up coffee cup, and the cats were settled with food and toys, River filled their water dishes in the bathroom.

When they returned, Rye was playing with the kitten named Orange and someone had claimed the red-draped table next to theirs.

The *Reserved* card and the candy cane were gone. In their place was a heavy wooden sign that appeared to be hand-carved. But River couldn't focus on the handiwork, because all they could see was the word *TAXIDERMY*. And on the table beside it, staring up at them, was the mounted head of a buffalo.

"Jesus fucking Christ."

"I know," Rye said. "Like, did they put us next to each other because we both deal with animals?"

"I don't know if that's logical or ghoulish."

"Why choose? Hey, okay, just try this, would you?" He held out a traveler mug of coffee. "Please, just one sip? I don't get it."

Rye had a particular expression at times that made him look like a lost little boy.

River took the coffee from him and sipped.

Instantly, they regretting being susceptible to people's feelings.

"Okay, that's not a good face," Rye said. "Just, like, I'm a good cook!"

He was.

"I make good cocktails."

He did. *Very* strong, but good.

"But you all hate my coffee and I feel like I'm losing my mind because it tastes totally normal to me."

"I don't know, Rye, it's just bad. It's too bitter, it tastes a little burnt, and it makes my tongue sad."

River shook his head slowly and took the mug back.

"Here, taste mine," River offered.

Rye took a sip from their thermos.

"This tastes like candy," he said.

"It tastes like correctly brewed coffee with cream and sugar in it."

River said, "You can *put* cream and sugar in this coffee, I just don't like it that way."

"Well, fortunately you run a cat shelter and not a coffee shop, so maybe let's leave the coffee to Cameron and focus on the cats."

Rye muttered something under his breath, but got back to setting up the display. River went in search of the bag full of toys they'd brought, and realized they'd left it in the van.

"I'll be back in a minute," they told Rye.

The bag was caught under the seat and River extracted it with a triumphant yank.

The bag came free, but they teetered backward right along with it, bracing for the impact of the icy pavement. But it didn't come. Instead, they smacked into something a lot warmer and a lot more animate.

"Oh, shit, I'm so sorry," they said to whomever they'd just body-checked.

"You all right, River?"

They looked up to see that the person they'd run into was none other than Cassidy Darling.

In the light, he was stunning. Strong brows and a straight nose and that beard that made him look dapper as hell.

Cassidy looked down at them with those intelligent brown eyes, just like he had at the cat shelter last week and all the sounds in the parking lot faded into the background. All they could feel was the pounding of their heart.

"Yeah. Sorry," River said.

"Good. How's the cat?"

True to their word, River had texted Cassidy the morning after he brought the cat in to let him know that the vet said it looked like she was going to be fine. His hearty and quick response was, *Excellent! I'm so glad to imagine her safe with you.*

It was possible that River might have looked at it a couple of times in the intervening week.

"She's doing well. That little tip of her ear that Molly thinks was frostbitten has fallen off and she didn't even seem to notice."

Cassidy smiled warmly at the news.

"Good."

River stood, unsure what to say next. When nothing came to mind, they locked the van and turned to walk back toward the convention center. Cassidy walked with them.

"And how are you?" he asked.

"Pretty good. I'm here with the shelter, trying to get cats adopted. Only it turns out our table is next to some Daniel Boone weirdo who stuffs animals for fun. So when children are playing with one of the cute little kitties, they can look over and imagine it being stuffed and its head mounted on someone's wall."

River wasn't quite awake yet and that comment had come out snarkier than they'd intended.

"Anyway, what are you doing here? Are you a Craftmas superfan?"

River was mostly joking—Cassidy wasn't dressed in red and green, nor did he sport any novelty Christmas accessories. But then again, the same could be said of River.

"I am a fan," Cassidy said slowly. "It's my most lucrative event of the year."

Thank god. River hadn't thought Cassidy seemed the type, but they reminded themself that they didn't actually know anything about him.

"Oh, that's cool. What do you vend?"

Cassidy waited a moment before responding. The sun glinted in his nose ring and picked out some red strands in his hair.

"Taxidermy," he said.

CHAPTER 4

Cassidy

Once, Cassidy Darling had experienced the displeasure of telling a friend he'd seen his boyfriend making out with someone else at a bar. There was a moment when his friend's whole face collapsed, like mortification and despair had the power to leave marks on his physical reality.

River's face was a surprisingly similar mask of mortification and despair. Their wide blue eyes bugged out in horror, their mouth gaped, and their forehead knotted.

"Ohmygod, fuck. I'm ... I ... I didn't ... Fuck."

They twisted the handles of their canvas bag around their hands so tightly he worried they'd injure themself.

"Don't worry about it," Cassidy started to say, but before he could, River turned tail and scampered away.

Once all his pieces were loaded in and his table set up, Cassidy went back outside. It was thirty minutes until the doors opened and already there was a line that snaked through the parking lot. This was his last bit of comfort before he'd be subject to the fluorescent lights in the convention center for three solid days.

Migraines were the cost of vending there, unfortunately. He'd made sure he was rested and hydrated in an attempt to slightly mitigate the effects, but that was all he could do.

Cassidy had been excited to realize his table was next to the cat shelter's and he might see River. Their brief interaction the week before had piqued his curiosity. Hell, they were gorgeous, interesting, and adorably awkward—what wasn't to like?

The truth was, he understood why some people didn't like taxidermy, especially someone who worked with live animals. He hadn't expected that level of scorn from River, though.

He'd just have to hope that once they became more familiar with it, River could see past his craft's stereotypes to the art of it— at least enough to keep getting to know him.

Because Cassidy definitely wanted to get to know River. And he only had the three days of Craftmas to make it happen.

Okay, it's time to debut CANDLEDERMY!

The text from Cassidy's sister, Nora, came ten minutes before they opened the doors and was his cue to get back to their table.

"I'm still not sold on that name," he told her as he approached.

The table looked marvelous. Nora had taken care in hanging the larger pieces on the wall behind the table and displaying the pieces with flat bases on a pyramid of wooden boxes that Cassidy had built new for this year.

Their newest collaborations commanded the table.

Nora was a chandler, and both she and Cassidy hated for anything to go to waste. So they'd had the idea to combine their crafts: the fat that Cassidy removed from animals during the taxidermy process could be rendered for candles, and the bones became the material for candle holders, candelabras, and other similar decor.

The first time they'd tried the rendered fat, they candles had ended up too liquid, so Nora began experimenting with different ratios, mixing the fat with beeswax she bought from a beekeeper in New Orleans. After much trial and error, she found a ratio that produced a sturdy candle that burned with the sweet scent of beeswax.

Her designs began simply: turning an elk's rib into a candlestick or a curve of skunk vertebrae into a menorah. Then she began to combine the materials with her metalworking skills, and something unique was born: candlescapes that were usable art.

One of Cassidy's favorite pieces had begun as a long piece of fallen wood. On one side, Nora had attached a terra cotta planter that held a small cactus; on the other side, the delicate bones of a hawk's wing curled around a metal cactus blossom, at the top of which was a metal holder and a tall, wide candle tinted sage green. It would be just as gorgeous as the centerpiece for a dinner party table as it would sitting on a windowsill.

"I'm still not sold on that term," he told Nora. "But the booth looks great. Thanks for taking the lead on that."

"Why not?"

"Because, the *-dermy* part of taxidermy means skin, so without the *taxi-* part, which means arrangement, it's like you're calling them skin candles, which sounds creepy. And inaccurate."

Nora rolled her eyes.

"You know people just like an evocative portmanteau, right? They're not actually parsing the Greek and Latin root words to see if the etymology is sound. Besides, *Taxicandles* sounds like an emergency product you keep in your pocket in case your Lyft is too dark and *Dermicandles* sound even *more* like creepy skin candles."

Cassidy couldn't argue with that.

"Um." She leaned close. "What's the deal with Jumpy over there?"

She inclined her head slightly to River, who had been keeping conspicuously busy since Cassidy had walked up.

"Let's get a coffee before the crowd descends," he suggested amiably.

As soon as they were out of earshot, Nora hissed, "Did you sleep with our Craftmas neighbor?"

"What? No! They're the one I was telling you about. River. Who I brought the cat to."

"Oh, right. So they're just being weird because they had the displeasure of hanging out with you?"

She grinned and shoulder checked him.

"Haha. They, uh, aren't the biggest fan of taxidermy, I think. They don't like the idea of kids coming to adopt a kitten and imagining it stuffed on someone's wall."

"Pshh, kids think about the weirdest shit all the time. Buck Slater's kid told me I was a demon at the grocery store the other day."

"How did she figure it out?"

"I know, right?" Nora winked at Cassidy and whisked their coffees to the register where she paid for both.

"Thanks."

Nora caught Cassidy's elbow and turned him to face her.

"Listen. This is going to be great for us. We've never had the whole year to prepare before, and we didn't have the capacity to take custom orders on the spot. Now that we do, we can actually see if this will be sustainable."

Cassidy nodded, visions of a dozen new projects he wanted to start already dancing in his head. His head, which was already throbbing from being in the fluorescent lights for an hour. The devastation that he'd feel when he dragged himself home tonight— to say nothing of the two days that would follow—was a guarantee, and he tried to push it from his mind.

"And that means that I need you to be a hundred percent."

"Huh? Oh, yeah, of course. What?"

"Cass ..." She bit her lip. "Just, please focus on our booth, not on the cat kid. Okay? I know how you are."

"And how am I, exactly?" he sniffed.

"Don't get upset, I'm not saying you're gonna do anything wrong. Just that ..."

Her face cycled through expression after expression, like she was searching for a non-devastating way to announce his failings as a person.

"Jesus, just say it, Nor."

"You have a tendency to get a bit distracted when you're focusing on someone you have the hots for. I know you can't help it. It's not a bad thing. It would just be terrible timing if it happened this weekend. You know?"

Cassidy nodded.

"Yeah, fine."

Nora wasn't wrong. ADHD was something that he'd been dealing with since before he was diagnosed at ten. For the past twenty years he'd experienced what it meant to have a brain that didn't work with the ways the world was set up. And, yeah, one of the things his brain loved to do was to fixate on new people as he met them.

There were so many questions and they were all so interesting that sometimes hours would pass in conversation or thought without his notice, leaving him in a position where he needed to scramble to keep the rest of his life in order.

Still, Nora being correct didn't make it feel any better to be reminded of the capacity his brain had to ruin their collective lives.

"I'm sorry, C. It's just—"

"I know, dude. Don't worry about it. It's under control."

He didn't add, *Because they probably want nothing to do with me now that they think I'm an animal murderer.* Some things, he'd learned the hard way, didn't need to be said aloud.

Nora squeezed his shoulder and they headed back to the table, sipping their very bad coffees.

For a moment, the Christmas music that was piped through every speaker in the building quieted and a nasal voice announced, "Attention vendors, staff, and volunteers, the doors are opening now. Repeat, the doors are now opening and guests will be inside shortly."

Nora and Cassidy turned to one another. This weekend could make the difference between them being able to keep making art full time and having to go back to the jobs they'd left the year before.

"Here," Cassidy said, "goes nothing."

CHAPTER 5

Cassidy

The first rule of Craftmas was: people don't know what they want until you tell them. The second rule of Craftmas was: if they think they don't want what you're selling, tell them to gift it.

"Hello!" Cassidy would call to people passing the table. "Do you like ethical taxidermy?"

And like clockwork, they'd ask what made it ethical, leaving an opening for him to tell them about how he didn't hunt, trap, or kill any animals. Instead, he found animals that had died already (he'd learned the first year never to say the word *roadkill*) or that people found and brought to him. He told them that he and Nora were now able to use many other parts of any animal he mounted in her candles.

Nora would offer people the matchbooks she'd made with the Candledermy logo and use the freebies to draw them into conversations about the candles. Very few people could resist a freebie.

After a few hours they had the demographics nailed down. They could tell at a glance if someone would be more likely to care about candles or taxidermy and hail them accordingly.

Many of the men that attended Craftmas were there with partners or families, so Cassidy appealed to them because he looked like them, and they came over to check out his work, bringing their families with them. Nora would then sell the rest of the family on her candlescapes if they weren't in the market for something as expensive as taxidermy.

Nora's work was creating interest, with multiple people having ordered bespoke pieces already. She'd been delighted to find that there was a vein of Craftmas attendees of the *Nightmare Before Christmas* ilk, and they were all drawn to her iron and bone altar candlesticks and candelabras.

They also had an unexpected runaway hit with Nora's vertebrae taper candle holders. They were her least expensive offering, and quick to make, so when she sold out by midday, she promised people that she'd make more tonight and have them restocked the next day.

"Should I leave now and start making them?" she asked.

"Yeah, okay. And I can come to your place tonight and help out so we have enough for tomorrow."

"Great, and remember to tell people that the candles don't release any toxins or pollutants into the air the way paraffin candles do, and that there's no lead in the wicks, and they're all natural, and—"

Cassidy put a hand on her shoulder. "I know the specs, I promise."

She saluted, threw on her coat, and left him to run the booth himself. And he was glad of it five minutes later when a white guy in a T-shirt that announced *I'm Not Santa but You Can Sit in My Lap* approached and started giving him shit about the "ethical" part of ethical taxidermy.

Nora was what their parents had always called "spirited," which meant that she didn't take any shit and she wasn't scared of people thinking she was weird. It was a gift.

"You gotta say that part because of the woke police, huh?" he said, trying to bro down with Cassidy.

"Nope," he said, keeping a smile on his face and his voice

neutral. "I say that part because I believe in it. Now, let me show you some of the pieces that *most* people can't appreciate ..."

This disarmed the man, as it usually did. People like this asshole were instantly won over by being told they were superior to others in any way.

River had conspicuously ignored Cassidy for the first two hours of Craftmas. They'd glanced over many times, but when Cassidy met their gaze or turned toward their table, they suddenly turned around to tend to one of the cats.

Finally, there was a slight lull and Cassidy stepped up to the shelter's table.

"How's the adoption search going?"

"Um, it's good, I guess?" River said, staring at the floor. "I have no baseline, really. It's the first time we've done this. Yellow got adopted, though."

"Which one was Yellow?" Cassidy asked.

"The little gray kitten."

Their voice was soft in the din, and Cassidy took a step closer to hear them. River turned away and started tidying the stack of brochures on the table. For a moment Cassidy thought they couldn't get over the awkward exchange a few hours before, but when he really looked at River he could see that their eyelashes were spiky with moisture.

Fuck, they were teary because they were going to miss the kitten. Cassidy's stomach twisted up toward his heart.

They shook their head almost violently, like they could banish the emotion, but a tear slipped down their cheek and they turned to him, probably only to avoid being seen by the crowd.

"Hey, it's okay," Cassidy began.

"I know it's stupid. The *whole* point of being here is to get them placed in good homes. I just ..." They trailed off and scrubbed at their eyes. "Anyway, I'm gonna ..."

They turned to a kid who was looking brightly at the two remaining cats and to her parents who looked cautiously optimistic. Cassidy left them to it.

But the tension had eased between the two tables and after that River didn't shy away from acknowledging him. When the fourth person sung the praises of the gingerbread cookies at the bakery booth three tables down, Cassidy popped over and bought a few.

He held out one of the cookies to River when he returned.

"I got you a gingerbread man if you can bear to bite his head off."

River raised an eyebrow as they unwrapped the cookie.

"You don't know their gender or pronouns," they said flatly.

Cassidy's stomach clenched with guilt.

"Oh, shit, you're right, I shouldn't assume."

He felt terrible. Of all the silly, normative things to say about a *cookie*.

But River grinned.

"I'm fucking with you," they said, and bit the head off the gingerbread cookie. "Damn. That's really good. Thanks."

"You're welcome," Cassidy said absently. He couldn't tear his eyes away from their mouth. He liked feeding them. And he decided not to examine why very closely.

By mid-afternoon, Cassidy was in hell.

His fluorescent light sensitivity had begun several years before, and had only intensified since then. Now, even five minutes in a fluorescent-lit place was enough to catalyze the reaction.

First, it felt like his eyeballs were vibrating. Next, it felt like someone was gouging them out with a grapefruit spoon. Then, a band of pressure around his head like a vise. Finally, the nausea, which would have him vomiting if he stayed in them too long.

All the symptoms intensified the more sleep-deprived or dehydrated he was, and the more sensory input he was getting in addition to the fluorescents. He'd rested the night before, had a huge water bottle with him at the table, and was doing his best to eat at regular intervals.

Still, with each hour that passed he felt worse and worse. He'd known he would—this was the third year that he and Nora had attended Craftmas. Nora had even offered to do the event on her own so he wouldn't get zapped, but it was too big a job for either of them on their own.

No matter how cheesy the event was—and it was *extremely* cheesy, because it was a Christmas craft fair—it was also joyous and energizing and Cassidy enjoyed talking to the people who were interested in the booth, not to mention all the other vendors.

But even though he had gone into the day with his eyes open, those same eyes were now asking things like *But why would you want to gouge us out with grapefruit spoons? What'd we ever do to you?* His stomach, though pleased with the deposit of a cookie, screamed *What's the point? You're just gonna puke it up.* And his head added very good points as well, such as *I will still ache tomorrow, just FYI.*

Cassidy thought he was doing a good job of keeping the discomfort off his face—at least, none of the customers seemed to notice anything. But the next time there was a lull, River grabbed his hand and tugged him toward the bathrooms.

When they were out of view of the crowd, they said, "What the hell is going on with you? You look like you're about to faint. Are you sick? What's up?"

Somewhere, deep in his nauseated gut, River's concern was a cool breeze of mint against the burning roil. *They noticed I was ill! They noticed and they cared!*

Okay, loverboy, he heard Nora's voice say in his head. *Basic human kindness isn't exactly a declaration of love. Take it down a notch.*

"I'm kind of allergic to fluorescent lights."

"Allergic to ... " River looked up. "But *all* the lights in here are fluorescent."

"Yeah."

"Oh my god, what's *wrong* with you?"

"A lot, probably."

River ignored his flippancy.

"Most immediately?"

"Uh." Cassidy scanned his body. His eyes felt like they were popped out of his head and his optic nerves were vibrating, like if Dali had made that melting clock painting about eyeballs. His head was being crushed by a vice of pain. But there was nothing that would help there.

"Puking," he said.

"You need to, or you're trying to avoid it?"

It was such an infinitely complex question that would take so much information to explain.

Into the silence of Cassidy's overwhelm, River simply said, "Close your eyes and come with me."

Cassidy didn't even try to argue, just closed his eyes, begged his body to hold up for a few more hours, and focused on the single spot of good feeling in his body: his right hand, which was in River's as they pulled him along.

The frosty winter air hitting his face was an intense relief. Yeah, it also smelled of cigarette smoke, exhaust, and generic parking lot goo, but the sudden cold shocked his system a bit, distracting from his discomfort.

He gulped in deep, refreshing breaths, trying to smell nothing but the snow and trees. It would only be a temporary fix; his symptoms would come back the moment he went inside. But the break seemed to have quieted his gag reflex if nothing else, for which he was grateful.

"Thanks," he said on a sigh. "I'd better get back in, though."

River nodded. They were shivering in the cold without a jacket.

"Is there anything I can do?"

It killed Cassidy to have to tell them no, there was nothing they could do. There was nothing anyone could do except realize that it was an accessibility issue for him and others (a *lot* of others, if the multiple subreddits he followed were any indication), and stop using them.

"You already did it," he said. "Thank you."

River nodded, but they were frowning.

"Okay. Let me know if you need anything?"

Cassidy promised that he would, filing away the look on their face to examine later.

"The doors are now closed," came the nasal announcement through the loudspeakers. "All guests should have exited the building now. Once again, all guests please exit the building. The doors will open again at nine tomorrow morning."

The last of the stragglers completed their purchases and trooped out, leaving the convention center a chaos of overflowing garbage cans, fallen seasonal cheer, and more mismatched gloves than a kindergarten lost-and-found.

Next to Cassidy, River slumped in exhausted, thank-god-I-can-stop-smiling relief. He'd witnessed two more of the cats get adopted that afternoon, and heard River tell a little girl who was disappointed that they didn't have what she'd called a "jam cat" (which her mother clarified meant an orange cat) that they'd have an orange tabby cat the next day. They'd kept their smile on the whole time, but now that it had fallen, the toll this was taking was evident.

"I'm sorry you'll miss them," Cassidy said.

He'd intended it to be quiet, intimate. But after needing to almost yell all day to be heard over the din, it came out much louder than he'd intended and they both winced.

"Thanks. I'm gonna probably go home and sit in the playroom with all the cats for a while."

"You have a lot of cats at home too, then?"

They looked confused for a moment, then shook their head. "I live at the cat shelter. Well, in an apartment above it. Same building. So I spend a lot of time with them. Too much, probably," they added.

"I know what you mean," Cassidy deadpanned. "Although all the animals I hang out with are dead."

River snorted with amusement.

"Yeah, listen, about that ..."

They looked at the wall, where a beautiful moose head with long lashes and glorious antlers hung.

"I'm sorry. About what I said earlier. I didn't know that your whole thing was *not* killing animals. And knowing that, they're really beautiful. I'm sorry I judged you."

"Don't worry about it," Cassidy said. "I'm not."

That was true. It was plain that River had spoken out of care for animals and he'd never be angry at someone for that.

They smiled and went back to packing up the cats' accoutrements.

"Do you need help getting everything to the parking lot?" he asked.

All he wanted in the entire world was to lie down in a dark room, but he couldn't seem to bring himself to take leave.

"No. Thanks, though. I've got the shelter van right outside. You should get out of these lights."

"I think I will. See you tomorrow." And then, for no reason that his conscious mind could justify, what came out of his mouth next was, "Sleep well, River."

Something like panic or desire flashed in River's eyes for a moment and then was gone.

"Okay," they said.

CHAPTER 6

River

"Is that you guys?" River called toward the dark playground. They should've brought a flashlight. The light in their phone did little to cut through the rural winter dark.

"Nooo," came a lilting, spooky voice from near the shadow of the play structure, "Ve vant to suck your bloooooood."

"Well, thank goodness someone does."

They walked in the direction of the voice. As they approached, they could just see the cherry of Nate's cigarette burning a hole in the darkness.

Nate was reclining on top of the metal play structure and Tracy was a few rungs below, legs wound through the bars. She jumped down like a giant spider and skittered toward River.

"You have arrived, Oh Holy One," she intoned—a joke left over from high school, when River wore every garment they owned to holes and tatters. A few curls of her blonde hair poked out the bottom of her knit hat and glitter streaked her eyebrows, twinkling in the moonlight.

"I dunno if we can hang out here anymore," River said. "I kinda feel like a creep."

"It's not like there are kids here," Nate said, shrugging and slithering off the play structure. He threw an arm around River's shoulders in a casual hug. "Hey, Riv."

He offered River a cigarette, which they declined. He took a metal cigarette case from his other pocket and opened it to reveal four perfectly rolled joints.

"Bless you, my child," River said, plucking a joint from the case and lighting it off Nate's cigarette.

"How's the big city?" they asked Nate. "I thought you weren't getting back into town until Christmas."

Nate had left for Los Angeles in September, determined to break into special effects in the movie industry.

A shadow crossed Nate's usually placid face.

"Yeah, I uh. I don't think that's gonna work out." He chewed his lower lip, a habit River hadn't seen him do for years. "There's no way to get hired unless you know someone in the business and there's no way to meet people in the business unless you, like, already know someone in the business. Or sleep with them. Or do drugs with them. Which, sign me up, but *how*?"

He shook his head and lit a joint. Tracy took it from him for a few hits and passed it back.

"Are you gonna—"

"Honestly, I don't wanna talk about it, okay?"

River nodded. It was a firm rule among them that they all respected.

"You want to hear about how I'm a total bonehead instead?" River asked.

"Always," said Tracy.

"You? Impossible!" Nate said.

"Har har har." River glared at Nate, but the weed was making things soft around the edges and unknotting the snarl their stomach had been in since that morning.

They told Nate and Tracy the story of meeting Cassidy at the shelter, then accidentally insulting him to his face.

Nate frowned. Tracy's eyes widened in horror.

"A Daniel Boone weirdo who stuffs animals for fun?" she repeated, dissolving into laughter.

"Wait, is that the coonskin cap dude?" Nate asked.

"I think that's Davy Crockett?" Tracy said.

"It is. I googled it after," River muttered. "And Daniel Boone owned slaves, so clearly he's awful in ways that had nothing to do with killing every animal he could. And I compared Cassidy to him."

"Oh no," Tracy groaned mockingly. "You compared a straight white man to another straight white man who was a hunting slave-owner; how will he *ever* recover from the inaccuracy and injustice? Please."

She blew out a scornful raspberry.

"I actually ... kinda ... maybe think he's not totally straight," River said haltingly.

"Reaaaally," Nate said just as Tracy said, "How can you tell?"

River sighed. This was a source of exquisite discomfort for them and they were still working on how to explain it without a bunch of gender shit that felt bad.

River was nonbinary, so when people expressed attraction to them, they couldn't really draw any conclusions about what that might say about people's sexual orientation. Not that anyone could, for that matter, but it was especially difficult for River to parse people's attraction to them. Which was fine, in practice, but when it came to attempts to speculate about whether feelings were requited, it left something to be desired.

"He told me to sleep well."

"When?" Nate asked.

"Today. This afternoon. Evening. At Craftmas."

"What time was it exactly?" asked Tracy.

"Um, doesn't matter," Nate said. "Dudes don't just tell random people they *aren't* thinking about romantically or sexually to sleep well. Doesn't happen."

"Surely it must happen *sometimes*?" Tracy said.

Nate gawked at her. "Do *you* go around randomly telling people to sleep well?"

She opened her mouth and then closed it.

"That's what I thought. You say that to children, old people, and people you're dating. The end."

"Also, he bought me a cookie. A gingerbread cookie."

"Okay," Nate drawled. "That could go either way."

"Yeah, some people are weirdly friendly," Tracy agreed. "Remember when Letitia Barrington paid my bar tab for no reason?"

River and Nate exchanged a look.

"Um, dude. Letitia Barrington didn't want you to get arrested for underage drinking so she paid your tab to get you the hell out of the bar."

"Plus," Nate added, "she totally wanted to bone you."

"She ... no she didn't. Did she?"

"She absolutely did," River confirmed.

"But ... but ... she's a *librarian*." Tracy spat out *librarian* as if she were saying *priest*.

"I think they repealed that law that said librarians weren't allowed to experience attraction," River said.

"Shut up," Tracy grumbled. "Well, damn. Why didn't y'all tell me earlier."

"Cuz it was completely obvious and we assumed you knew?" Nate said.

"Because you were still with Betsy," River corrected. Then they grinned and added, "And because it was completely obvious and we assumed you knew."

"Damn, missed opportunity," said Tracy.

"Not like she's dead," Nate said with a shrug.

"Anyway, can we pivot from my pathetic obliviousness back to River's?"

"Yes." Nate looked at River seriously. "You know what you have to do? Make it up to him."

Visions fell unbidden into River's mind: dropping to their

knees before Cassidy and apologizing; bringing him breakfast in the morning and watching him eat it; kissing a slow trail from his anklebone to his throat.

They shook their head to clear it.

"Uh. Make it up to him how?"

Tracy and Nate shared a smile.

"I'm sure you'll figure it out."

CHAPTER 7

River

R iver had psychedelic video game dreams that they were still trying to wake up from when they got to the convention center to set up for the second day of Craftmas. That was what happened when you stayed up stupid late trying to defeat the Soul Tyrant in *Hollow Knight* while cats crawled all over you because you didn't want the morning to come when you'd have to say goodbye to some of them.

Their stomach lurched at the sight of Cassidy already at his table when they got there. Nora, whom River had learned was Cassidy's sister, was buzzing around, arranging the table and muttering to herself. Cassidy, two steps up a ladder, seemed to be able to tell which of her mutterings were actually directed at him and responded accordingly. Must have been a sibling thing.

"Hey," River said, setting the cat carriers down.

It was barely audible in the echoey room with Christmas music already blaring. Nora didn't respond. But Cassidy turned, his whole face brightening when he saw River.

"Good morning," Cassidy boomed. Then he winced.

Upon closer observation, there were dark hollows around Cassidy's eyes and his skin looked sallow. But his smile seemed genuine and his brown eyes sparkled.

"I um."

Casual, River. Be casual, not weird. Casual, not *weird.*

"Can I show you something?"

Cassidy stepped down from the ladder in a single lunge.

"Yeah, show me something."

"Oh, well, it's not a big deal. Just."

They pulled their phone out and swiped to the picture they'd taken late last night.

Cassidy peered at the photo of the small tabby cat twisted into a pretzel mid-groom, tongue out and yellow eyes half closed, and smiled.

"That's her, huh? She looks like she's doing okay."

"She is. I thought maybe, since you found her, saved her life, that you might want to name her?"

"I'd be honored," Cassidy said.

He took River's phone and zoomed in closer on the cat in the picture, seeming to study her.

"Inspector Gadget."

"What?"

Cassidy nodded in confirmation.

"How come?"

River wanted to understand what Cassidy saw in the cat to choose that name.

"Oh, uh: cat, villain petting a cat, James Bond, *Get Smart, Inspector Gadget.* Did you ever see it? It's from the eighties."

River shook their head and IMDBed it.

"My dad used to get it from the library for me, Nora, and Silas. He loved James Bond movies and I think he was trying to get us excited to watch them by showing it to us."

"To his great disappointment, it never worked," Nora said while spacing candles equally across one side of the table.

"Is Silas your other sibling?"

Nora and Cassidy exchanged glances. Cassidy nodded, brow furrowed. Nora moved a candle one centimeter to the left and looked critically at the display.

"You don't have to ..." River said quickly.

"No, it's ... We don't really have contact with Silas if we can help it."

"*I* can always help it," Nora said.

Cassidy squirmed. "Yeah, I'm not as good at it."

River was curious by nature. For a long time, they'd tried to stifle that curiosity beneath a studied neutrality. Many people, they'd learned early, treated interest as weakness they could exploit. If people knew the things you were interested in, they drew conclusions that were beyond your control. If they knew the things you valued, they could devalue them, and you by extension.

It had always been important to keep these things private, especially around their father. And it hadn't been until Rye had given them a place that was their own—a safe, private place that no one had the ability to invade—that River'd had the space and privacy to determine what their interests were. Curiosity, they realized, was only a weakness to those who were threatened by its inevitable results: education, expansion, connection.

Slowly, over the last two years, River had allowed their curiosity to reintroduce itself.

"What's his deal?" they asked.

"He's ..." Cassidy stroked his beard.

It looked soft. River wondered what it would feel like against their lips if they leaned in and kissed Cassidy on the cheek. If it would rasp against their skin if Cassidy kissed them.

"He's a cop," Nora said. "And he's every kind of fucked up that being a cop entails."

"Oh, yikes. ACAB," River said.

"Yeah. And little peacemaker Cass tries to rehabilitate him every chance he gets, to no avail."

"I'm not trying to rehabilitate him, just share all the reasons why I and other people want to abolish the system of policing. But he's our brother and it's not so easy for me to believe that he's beyond hope. I think people can change if you give them the chance. Don't you?"

The hope in his eyes made River wish so desperately that they agreed. Nora clearly had no such compunction. She rolled her eyes and went back to readying the table.

"I think," River said carefully, "that change is possible. But it's the end result of a lot of work and time, and I've found most people aren't interested in doing that kind of work unless they're about to lose something they truly feel they can't live without."

Cassidy looked like he wanted to query that, but the announcement over the loudspeaker telling them the doors would open in thirty minutes sent Cassidy, Nora, and River scrambling to prepare for the crowd like everyone else.

CHAPTER 8

Cassidy

Cassidy didn't have time to think about Silas for even a moment after the doors opened, and for this he was grateful.

He'd spent the previous evening helping Nora assemble more vertebrae candle holders, despite the fact that by the time he'd gotten home from Craftmas his head had felt like a piñata at the end of a birthday party.

"You look like boiled shit," Nora had said when he came into the studio she'd set up in his guest room. "You should go to bed. I got this."

Cassidy waved her off. "It'll be a good distraction."

Rest, she was right, was the only thing that could ameliorate his symptoms—if however slightly—but rest was also the thing that gave him a chance to concentrate on them. On how his body felt, how it should feel, and the vast, ungovernable space between. Besides, he'd just get zapped by the fluorescents the next two days anyway.

No, resting wasn't on Cassidy's to-do list until Craftmas was over. Then he could nurse the postdrome in a haze of NyQuil and solitude because no one would need him. No one would be depending on him. He wouldn't have to try and hide his misery for the comfort of the people who loved him.

They'd made candle holders until Nora's fingertips blistered and the box that held vertebrae was empty, and then made a sign with a scannable QR code that led to a page on Nora's website where they would direct people to place orders in case they sold out again.

Now, as the doors opened and the second day of Craftmas began, Cassidy flipped the switch in his brain that relegated his physical discomfort to a background sensation by way of accepting that he *had* to be here and there was no way out of his pain. Cassidy had learned a long time ago that necessity was the mother of dissociation and, much like his own mother, could not be reasoned with, so he didn't try.

From the moment the doors opened, the energy was electric. Day one of Craftmas was for first timers, casual enthusiasts, and locals. But day two was the make or break—the day when people who scouted the booths on day one were now ready to buy; the day groups of friends who'd attended for years came in unique DIY costumes or matching Christmas shirts found on Etsy or Target or Walmart or Amazon and therefore identical to everyone else's.

There were bachelorette party-style tiaras and sashes with rhinestone announcements on them, jingle bells attached to every imaginable surface, sweaters and scarves and hats that made Cassidy felt overly warm just by looking at them.

These groups insisted on taking pictures with the crafts, costumes, and people they liked, which was how Cassidy found himself the unofficial photographer of The Dirt Road Cat Shelter's adoptable cats whenever he wasn't telling people about his work.

He took pictures of so many people with the cats that he started to get annoyed that they were treating living creatures like props. But River didn't seem to mind as long as the cats didn't. As

Cassidy would hand back the cell phones, they would tell people to tag the shelter when they posted the pictures on their socials.

"You never know what will make someone fall in love," they said after a couple in coordinated Santa and Mrs. Claus sweatshirts that announced, respectively, *I Do it for the Ho's* (which Cassidy was pretty sure wasn't grammatically correct), and *Santa's Favorite*, walked away in search of their next photo op.

They did not adopt the cat they took a picture with, an adorable black cat with a white band at its throat, named Priest. But a little boy who'd been watching them from a few feet away approached in their wake.

"Can I pet him?" the kid asked, and River, who was still holding Priest, crouched down so the kid could reach for the cat.

The kid held Priest tenderly to his chest and shivered with glee when Priest put a small paw on his shoulder.

"He likes you," River murmured.

The kid's face transformed into the face of someone who is liked, and something behind Cassidy's rib cage fluttered perplexingly. Before he had a chance to banish the feeling, much less figure out what it meant, two things happened: the loudspeaker screamed with feedback and the kid startled.

In that moment of distraction, Priest darted out of his grasp and disappeared into the sea of red and green.

The boy looked up at River, utterly horrified, and River returned the expression.

"I'm sorry," he said as an adult came over and put a hand on his shoulder.

"It's not your fault," River managed, but their wide eyes were panicked.

River peered into the crowd and took off in the direction Priest had gone. Cassidy took off after River.

"I'll help you," he offered.

River nodded absently, barely looking up as they stalked through the corridors, stooped and desperate, scanning.

"Have you seen a black cat?" Cassidy asked people. None of them had.

"Maybe he'll come back," Cassidy offered, placing a gentle hand on River's shoulder. River shrugged him off and kept walking.

Just then, Cassidy saw a tiny black fluffball dart between a display of Krampus ornaments and a busy fudge counter.

"There!"

He pointed and took off, River close on his heels. But within seconds the cat had disappeared once more into the crowd. River swore and spun around in a circle, looking.

"Damn," Cassidy said, trying to lighten the mood, "I guess Priest isn't in the mood to be held by any more confessors."

River did not appear amused. They stalked to the periphery where things were less crowded, and then toward a large door that stood half open so that people could pop out to the parking lot for a smoke or a breath of fresh air.

"Oh, fuck," River breathed. They ran for the door and stood peering out. "Shit, shit, shit."

"Hey, it's okay," said Cassidy.

"No it's fucking not," River snapped. "He could've wandered out here and gotten lost and it's freezing out."

Cassidy opened his mouth, hoping something reassuring might pop out.

"Good thing he's wearing a fur coat," is what his traitorous brain provided instead.

"It's seventeen fucking degrees out," River said. "And he's just a baby. Maybe you've never had to sleep outside in the middle of winter, but it fucking *sucks*."

River's eyes were haunted and their cheeks flushed. Then they were gone, leaving Cassidy in air cold enough that it could cut.

Cassidy swore and turned back inside. He had to find this fucking cat.

CHAPTER 9

Cassidy

After a quick wave from Nora that she'd hold down the fort, Cassidy began to search for Priest. There was no logic to where he began, but before long he realized that he should check all the places with food in the hopes the cat had smelled something good and gone in search. But neither of the food courts or the coffee stand revealed a cat.

On his rounds, he passed a booth that sold catnip mats in every color, and his heart leapt, certain he'd find Priest napping on one of them.

"Has a cat been sitting on these?" Cassidy asked.

The person behind the booth looked confused. "Well, I make them at home and I have two cats. So probably they've sat on some of them at one point or another. Is your cat quite territorial? Because I have some in a box that have never—"

Cassidy apologized and moved along. Crocheted stockings to hang with care; spiced nuts for that distant cousin who shows up when you didn't think they would; wine bottle gift bags elaborate enough to make spirits more than something you give to the coworker who has a shabby chic *Live, Laugh, Wine* decorative wood block on their desk.

No sign of Priest.

Past blown glass ornaments and stained-glass wreaths; past a child reaching for the ear of a service dog and the chaos that ensued; past a woman grabbing truffles off a tray and being told they weren't free samples but eighteen dollars' worth of merchandise, Cassidy searched.

Still no sign of Priest.

Past carolers in matching sweaters and the facade of a snowy cabin hung with mistletoe and holly; past a woman with her eyes closed, taking deep, calming breaths as two kids in braids tugged on her sweater and made demands.

No Priest.

Cassidy started to feel the concern he'd dismissed in River. What if the sweet little cat *had* gotten outside. What if, confused and perhaps fleeing the noise and fluorescent lights like Cassidy would so love to do, he had zigged instead of zagged and now couldn't find his way back to the booth? What if, as Cassidy was driving home that evening, he passed a small black form lying motionless on the side of the road?

"Fuck, fuck, fuck," he muttered through gritted teeth.

A white woman wearing a sweater with Santa on it that declared *I Have a Big Package For You*, gave him a dirty look. He grimaced and excused himself.

A murmur began in the crowd. Murmurs often began in the crowd at Craftmas—there were activities going on the whole time: contests for the best ugly Christmas sweater and the best rewrite of a classic carol, a cookie decorating demonstration and make-your-own-wreath classes. Murmurs usually meant a winner was being announced or a demonstration was beginning, so Cassidy ignored it and kept his eyes wide open for any sign of Priest.

But when the murmur turned to gasps and *Awws*, with phones being removed from pockets and purses and the bottom of bags loaded down with Craftmas goodies, Cassidy turned in the direction the phones were pointed.

The huge Christmas tree that was in the direct center of the room was ceremonially lit every day at noon, so Cassidy figured it was time for the lighting. But the event didn't usually include such wide-eyed stares from adults and children alike.

When a little boy next to him pointed at the top of the tree, Cassidy saw that it was ... Was it *moving*?

Yes, the boughs near the apex of the giant tree were rustling, the lights moving with them. Then, as Cassidy (and about two thousand other people) watched, a small head poked out of the tree and two fuzzy black ears pricked forward.

It was Priest, and he was yawning and attempting to make himself comfortable on the swaying bough a foot beneath the elaborate glass star that topped the tree.

He seemed utterly unconcerned about the crowd looking up at him and while people pulled out more and more phones to snap photos, Priest draped himself over the branch, rested his chin on his paws, and gazed lazily out at the crowd, as if he were people watching and had simply wanted the best vantage point.

The local news team, which always shot footage at the event for cheery human-interest stories, pointed their camera at the lavishly decorated tree. Cassidy could almost imagine what news anchor Tamara Michaelson would be saying. *Well, Gary, here's a question for you: who has two ears, four paws, and a ton of holiday spirit? The Christmas Cat, who has chosen the Craftmas tree as a home for the holidays.*

He snorted. Then he resigned himself to being the center of attention as he strode through the crowd toward the tree. He felt certain, somehow, that River would not wish to be the one to collect Priest in front of all these people.

There was a wide berth around the bottom of the tree—probably because the sight lines for a video weren't as good—and Cassidy met Jason, one of the tech people, at the base.

"Welp," Jason said.

"Yeah," Cassidy agreed. "Got a ladder?"

They did. In fact, the very tools that had been required to decorate the massive Fir were the tools that would help them get Priest. Between the two of them, they got a ladder set up beside the tree. By the time it was done, River ran over, cheeks flushed with cold and eyes watery.

"You found him?" they said, looking up at Cassidy, and he had such a strong urge to pull River to his chest, brush their hair back and reassure them, that he curled his hands into fists and shoved them in his pocket.

"Yeah. Guess he's not afraid of heights, huh?"

River shook their head, looking utterly undone.

"Don't worry," Cassidy said. "I'll get him."

It might as well have been the solemn pledge of a knight of the round table for all the determination with which Cassidy climbed the ladder. He would rescue the kitten, deliver it back into River's arms, and maybe earn a look or word of praise.

So preoccupied with this chivalric vision was Cassidy that he made it halfway up the ladder before it registered that he was climbing ... and that he was terrified of heights.

The vertigo hit Cassidy like a tidal wave. One second his brain hadn't caught up with his body's northward trek; the next, a rush of dizziness sent his head spinning and his stomach lurched into his throat. He closed his eyes against the disorientation, clinging so tightly to the ladder that the wood beneath his hands creaked in duress.

You are fine, Cassidy told himself in the most soothing tone his inner monologue could manage while halfway up a very tall ladder, in front of thousands of people, in an attempt to rescue a kitten, when he was already in a bad way from the effects of the fluorescent lights. *You are not going to faint or vomit or die. You are gonna move up to the next rung of the ladder one foot at a time and everything is going to be okay.*

Breathing shallowly through his nose, Cassidy opened his eyes and looked only up at Priest and moved slowly, rung by run, to the top of the tree.

He took a deep breath when Priest came into reach, and instantly regretted his failure to bring up something like a canvas bag or a blanket to wrap Priest in for the trip down the ladder.

Reaching out a slow hand to the kitten, not wishing to scare it, Cassidy got within a few inches of Priest's head when Priest disappeared into the tree.

The crowd gasped and Cassidy became aware that all their cameras, which had previously been pointed at Priest, were now aimed at him.

An unfortunate side effect of this awareness was that now that he'd looked down, Cassidy's vertigo was replaced with panic.

"Just don't puke," he murmured. "Please, please do not puke on the tree, or on the cat, or on all these people."

"Are you okay?" some well-intentioned guy dressed as one of Santa's elves called.

Unable to yell for fear of vomiting, Cassidy gave him a thumbs up sign and refocused on the task at hand.

"Priest. Come here, sweetie," Cassidy cooed.

He could just make out a soft meow over the din of the crowd. Clanging Christmas music still blasted from the loudspeakers and he could pick out individual voices from the crowd, which seemed to drill into his temples.

The excruciatingly heightened senses were another effect of the fluorescent lights. Soon, Cassidy knew, his nausea would become dry heaves, so he needed to get Priest and get the hell down this ladder before it began.

He called the cat's name, made kissy sounds and *Pspsps* sounds, but all to no avail. When he stuck an arm into the tree, hoping maybe he'd randomly hit fur, he knew he was getting desperate.

He swore and tried to gather his wits. There was nothing wrong with going down the ladder and sending Jason or someone in the crowd up. Maybe there was a veterinarian on the premises who'd know what to do. So why could he not make his foot move down to the next rung?

He was frozen. Cassidy wasn't sure how long he stood there, atop a ladder, his hand in a Christmas tree while thousands of people watched. But the next thing he knew, there was a soft voice below him saying, "Here," and handing him something.

It was River. Their blue eyes were locked on his and Cassidy opened his hand to find catnip and treats mingled on his palm.

Thank you didn't make it past his lips; he couldn't spare an iota of energy. As River made kissy noises and *Pspsps* sounds far superior to Cassidy's—they were a professional cat wrangler, after all—Cassidy eased his hand back into the tree, palm up, hoping Priest would want what he was offering.

River touched his knee gently, but Cassidy knew if he looked down again it would all be over—he was at his body's absolute limit. So he took deep breaths through his nose to stay in control..

"I don't need you to move or answer me or anything if you can't," River murmured. No one would be able to hear them over the din. "But you look really ill. And like you're gonna fall off this ladder. And I want you to not fall. So if there's anything I can do to help you not fall. I'd like to."

"Mmm," was all Cassidy could manage, but he thought River understood. There wasn't anything they could do. He would try not to fall. There was nothing else for it.

"Okay," River said. "Well, I'm gonna stay here."

Another grunt of affirmation and Cassidy knew he had to take a minute to get his body under control, because now if he fell he'd hit River on the way down.

"God dammit, Priest," River muttered. "I told Rye we shouldn't bring you."

Cassidy took deep breaths, and tried to name five things he could hear and smell. As he was noticing the smell of the plastic cording on the lights decorating the tree, a small, soft face butted into his hand, and the next thing he knew, a rough tongue swiped across his palm.

"Thank fuck," Cassidy breathed. River squeezed his knee.

"Do you want me to go get the cat carrier and bring it up?" River asked.

"Yeah," said Cassidy softly, not moving even an inch. Priest was now mouthing the treats, creeping closer to the ladder with each lick.

Relief swept through Cassidy, so cool and minty that for a moment Cassidy wondered if someone had opened a window in the ceiling and he was feeling fresh air gust through it.

"C'mere, baby," he encouraged the cat, and a cool nose pressed to his wrist.

Priest's head popped through the greenery and the crowd below exhaled as one.

"A local man has patiently waited at the top of the ladder," the anchor said in the prosody of all news anchors everywhere, "and it's just paid off. The Christmas cat has emerged."

Only the knowledge that it would make his head even worse kept Cassidy from rolling his eyes.

When he felt one little paw step on his palm, Cassidy knew he had to take this moment or miss it forever. If Priest stepped back off his hand and retreated into the center of the tree he might never find him again.

Just let go of the ladder and grab the damn cat! You won't fall— you're standing on solid wood.

He pried his sweating hand off the ladder and grabbed for the cat.

It didn't run back into the depths of the tree, for which Cassidy was quite grateful.

It did, however, dart in the other direction, and attach itself to Cassidy's chest, needle claws hooking in the thin cotton of his T-shirt.

The crowd gasped as one and Cassidy could almost write the lines for the newscaster: *Local man, barnacled by Christmas kitten, falls to his death at a holiday craft festival. The irony? He's a taxidermist, so maybe the cat thought turnabout was fair play.*

Then the comparatively insignificant pain from Priest's claws became more insistent, and Cassidy scanned the crowd for River, but they were nowhere in sight.

He couldn't wait for them, so he did the only thing he could think of. He reached down and pulled the hem of his shirt up and over the cat, then stripped it off over his head, quickly burritoing Priest.

More gasps, followed by laughter, and Cassidy clutched the writhing bundle to his chest.

"Please don't kill us," Cassidy asked Priest. "I can't die this way. Nora would never let me live it down."

Cassidy took the first step down the ladder, and all of Craftmas erupted into applause. His heart was thumping so hard against his ribcage that Cassidy worried it would explode, but he forced himself to take step after step. When the toe of his boot hit linoleum instead of wood, the crowd whooped with collective glee and he turned to find the news camera in his face.

"Local hero, Cassidy Darling, has brought the cat safely to the ground. Mr. Darling, what were you thinking as you took off your shirt to bundle this cat in? Were you thinking of the baby Jesus, wrapped in swaddling clothes and placed in a manger?"

"Uh," Cassidy said, head spinning. "No."

Then River was beside him, holding the cat carrier, eyes wide with relief.

"Thank you so much," they said over and over.

Cassidy tried to nod, but his body had reached its limit. As if they saw something in his eyes, River put a hand between his shoulder blades, cool and soft against his burning skin, and encouraged him through the crowd toward the bathrooms. Once shot of them, River took the bundle of Priest and Cassidy's shirt, untangled the cat, and deposited it in the cat carrier.

"You," River threatened Priest. But they didn't get any further than that. "And *you*."

For a second. Cassidy thought there was another cat that he hadn't noticed. Then he realized River was talking to him.

River handed his shirt back and Cassidy slipped it on.

"Excuse me for a moment," he managed, then he ran out the door to the parking lot and splattered the snow with coffee and stomach acid.

CHAPTER 10

River

R iver: *People, amirite?*
    Adam: *Aww, people are great! How was day 2? Make any friends??*
Adam: *Also remind me to tell you about how Gus almost got us banned from the new yarn store!*

R iver: *People, amirite?*
    Simon: *ugh, yes -__- you are right*
        River: *Any interest in thoroughly deriding humanity together?*
Simon: *only if it's over pie.*
River: *But of course.*

P each's Diner was a staple in Garnet Run. It didn't matter who you were or what you did, sooner or later you found your way there and once you had, you couldn't wait to return. The pie was great, yes. But Peach's was a place where you could hide in plain sight and people would usually leave you alone.

River had tea and pie ordered by the time Simon slid into the booth across from them, pulling off a gray and white knit hat with a yellow pom on the top.

He sketched a salute and River smiled.

Their friendship had happened slowly, and it was a relationship that River treasured. Simon had an anxiety disorder that made socializing hard for him. But since they'd first bonded over being the two people at every gathering who never said much, the relationship they'd struck up was one that valued ease and comfort and dispensed with the social niceties that neither of them valued.

Pie and tea were placed before them on the table: peach and jasmine for Simon and cherry and chamomile for River. Melba winked at Simon but said nothing and gave River a squeeze of the shoulder. Then she left them alone, as they preferred.

"So," River said. "The most horrible thing in the world has happened."

Simon's face asked, *Oh, god, what?*

"Ugh." River hid their face in their hands. "Ihaveacrush."

Oh no, Simon's face said. *Who?*

River groaned, took a bite of cherry pie and a sip of chamomile tea, and told him everything.

When they got to the part about the ladder and the Christmas tree, Simon's eyes widened.

"No shit? I saw that on the news," he said.

"What?!"

Simon snorted and pulled out his phone. When he handed it to River, the video on screen showed a shirtless Cassidy cradling a tiny bundle in his arms. His handsome face was creased with pain —although River doubted someone who wasn't looking for it would notice—and his muscles bulged. He looked for all the world like the hero on the cover of a romance novel.

River groaned.

"That's the guy?" Simon asked. "Jeez. Well. Uh. Wow."

"I know," River groaned. "It's pathetic."

Simon waved this away, but River knew he understood their

angst. One thing they appreciated about Simon was that he didn't engage in the kind of toxically cheery encouragements that some people meant well doing. He understood the basic realities of the universe, which were that people generally sucked and when they didn't you just had to stick around for a little while to see that they did.

"Okay, so how do I stop ... *you* know?"

Simon grimaced. "Well, after tomorrow you don't have to see him again, right?"

River nodded, the truth of that instantly deflating them.

"You don't wanna stop."

River shoved the last bite of pie in their mouth, letting the sweetness of sugar, the tartness of cherries, and the richness of butter mingle in their mouth in the perfect pie ratio.

That was what love should be like: disparate ingredients combining to produce something greater than any one was on its own.

"When I first met Jack," Simon said softly, leaning in, "he terrified me."

"He can definitely be a dick," River muttered.

Simon glared, eyes flashing, then allowed that, yes, he could be.

"It wasn't that, though," Simon said. "It was that he reminded me of all the people all my life who didn't have to experience what I experienced. I didn't trust that he had any context to understand me or my life."

Simon made sustained eye contact with River, something that didn't happen that often.

"What did you do?"

"Nothing. I was myself. Not that I had a choice," he added wryly. "I was myself and he was himself and slowly, through a lot of awkward shit—a *lot*, River—he kept trying to understand. And I kept trying to show him. And ..." Simon shrugged.

"That's it," River said, disappointed. "You were both yourselves."

"Well. Yes."

"You're useless to me, Burke," River said.

Simon grinned. "So I've heard." He scraped up his last bite of pie thoughtfully. "What's the issue?"

"You know. Shit's hard."

Simon nodded. He wasn't really someone you could bullshit, so River didn't try.

"Okay, so, um. I guess I don't know what his deal is with ... gender stuff? And me. And um. I dunno if he ... I dunno if we ... I just don't know if I ..."

"Right, sure, got it," Simon said.

"Shut up," River laughed. "Ugh, okay. He knows my pronouns and he's never misgendered me. Which is good. But I don't know how he thinks of me, or what his preferences are, and ... it just. Freaks me out."

Simon nodded.

"So sorry to be the bearer of bad news, but I think you have to talk it through with him."

"I was afraid you were gonna say that," River grumbled.

"Yeah, I know, it's the fucking worst."

"Another round to soften the blow of having to talk to people?" River asked.

"Definitely."

River went to the counter and got another piece of pie for each of them: blueberry for Simon and peach for River.

Pie procured, they looked at one another, and shared the deep sympathy that's the provenance of those who have to navigate atypical existences in a world that doesn't make space for them.

"I think it's a three-round problem," Simon said.

"I couldn't agree more," said River, and rose to procure a third slice of pie.

CHAPTER 11

River

The final morning of Craftmas dawned cold and sunny in Garnet Run, and as River woke, showered, dressed, and prepared for the day, they had imaginary conversations with Cassidy Darling.

By the time they saw the *real* Cassidy Darling, they figured, they'd be comfortable with him.

This was a method Simon had suggested the night before over their fourth round of pie. (It had proven to be a five-round evening and River had arrived home in good spirits and with a vague conviction that they should learn how to make pie.) He'd done it when getting to know Jack and they'd been blissfully happy together for three years now, so River was willing to try.

They had *not* expected that the real Cassidy Darling would roll up to his booth in worn black jeans that were frayed at the ankle where they hit work boots and clung to his ass, and a worn black T-shirt that seemed as if it'd shrunk slightly in the wash, so that the entire thing shifted when he moved, worn cotton slipping over smooth skin and rounded muscle like satin when he bent or stretched or twisted. The T-shirt had a small dot of bleach near the collar in the back and it had worn through to show skin beneath it.

The outfit made the words dry up on River's tongue and

bunch together, so that when Cassidy said hello and asked how their night had been, River said a string of words that concertinaed into an incomprehensible slab of sound.

They thought back to round five (pecan for River; key lime for Simon) and Simon's guide to how to be yourself in two steps. Step one: act like you would if you were alone; step two: when you realize that you can't act like you would if you were alone, get as close as you can.

River absently cursed Simon and attempted to turn back the sands of time so that they hadn't spoken at all.

"Sorry, what was that?" Cassidy asked politely, as if he had simply failed to hear River.

"Pie," was what came out of River's mouth then. And they threw a thumb's up sign in there for good measure. Clarity, that was really what it was all about.

"Pie," Cassidy echoed. "Pie sounds good."

River nodded miserably.

Soon after the doors opened to the public and capitalist pandemonium began, Simon and Jack approached, looking extremely out of place. Jack wore jeans and a black hoodie, his brown hair wild and his mien clearly communicating *Don't fuck with me.* Simon was holding his hand and seemed to have attempted to fit in by wearing a hand knit scarf in wild shades of green and pink.

River smiled thinking of him choosing it, saying, *Pink is basically red, but lighter.*

Simon was subtle and made for River with only a passing scan of everything to either side of them. Jack, had no such subtlety, giving Cassidy an up-and-down look that might've been a come on (if he hadn't clearly had eyes only for Simon) or a threat.

"Hello, River," Simon said. "Fancy meeting you here."

River almost laughed at how much effort he was putting into this display of casualness.

"Hey, River," Jack said, giving them a tight squeeze. "Just checking in to see if you need anything. You know. Because Rye asked us to."

Simon closed his eyes in *my-partner-is-bad-at-this*, and River could almost hear the conversation they must've had on the way here.

"Actually," River said, "I'm so glad you're here and I could use your help."

Jack's surprise was apparent. "You could?"

"That's what we're here for," Simon said quickly.

"So is that him?" Jack whispered too loudly as soon as they were huddled near the cats.

Simon elbowed Jack, then said to River, "I'm so sorry."

"Sorry for what? Sorry for me?" Jack asked.

Before River or Simon could reply, another familiar face appeared: Simon's grandmother.

"Hello, dears!" she trilled. "I've come to offer some help. What can I do?"

Her gaze drifted to the left to take in Cassidy and his booth.

"Jesus, did you put out a press release?" River hissed at Simon.

"Ummm ... It's possible that I might have made a mistake ..."

"Hello!" another familiar voice called, and Adam, Wes, and Gus burst through the crowd.

"I swear I didn't tell them," Simon hissed.

Charlie Matheson, Jack's older brother, was sauntering toward them from the other direction, towering over the rest of the crowd and looking like a younger, buffer Santa Claus.

"River!" he boomed.

"Oops," Jack said.

"Rye sent me to see if you needed any help with the cats," Charlie said. "Rye is my partner," he editorialized to Cassidy as if it was normal to announce such things to strangers.

Then he did a double take. "Oh, hey. You used to work with Dave, right?."

"That's right. Cassidy."

They shook hands and River and Simon exchanged looks.

"I didn't know they knew each other," Jack hissed. "Plus I forgot the dude's name when I was texting him."

Simon rolled his eyes and mouthed "Amateur hour" at River.

"Do you kill these animals?" Gus' voice cut through the din.

Adam and Wes were three steps behind. Cassidy bent down to see her.

"No, ma'am. I'm an ethical taxidermist. That means I don't kill anything."

"Are you a vegetarian?" was Gus' follow-up.

"No."

"Then you kill things all the time," she concluded, and turned away from him.

Adam slid a hand over her mouth and said tightly, "Remember how we discussed not casually accusing people of being killers?"

Gus shrugged. "Yes."

"Sorry," Adam said to Cassidy, who didn't seem offended.

"Oh jeez," Simon muttered.

River turned to see Zachary Glass and Bram Larkspur. Zachary was dressed in pressed blue trousers and a cream cable knit sweater —a casual outfit for him. Bram towered over him, a red and green knit hat pulled over his messy hair.

"Oh, hello, there, River. What a total surprise to run into you here, of all places."

Zachary's delivery was stiff and overly formal and Bram pressed his lips together to hide a smile.

"We thought we'd come offer you a hand with the cats," Bram said, clearly pleased with himself for coming up with this excuse.

Then he looked around and saw their entire friend group clustered around the cages.

"Ahh, I see. Um. Well. We're gonna walk around and look for, um, a Chanukah present for Zachary's parents."

"What? We said we're not seeing my parents for Chanukah," Zachary said as he was dragged off by the elbow.

River wished the floor would open up and swallow them whole. Barring that, perhaps another cat escape would create a diversion.

"I swear, I only told my grandma," Simon murmured in horrified shock. "Oh. I see what happened. Fuck, I'm s-so s-sorry."

With Simon's first stammer, Jack's arm came around him and pulled him close.

"It's my fault," he said. "Shoulda realized these nosy assholes would—"

"Do exactly what we're doing?" Simon finished, looking up at Jack.

Jack seemed to struggle to pull a frown and failed. He kissed Simon on the nose and seemed to forget about anything else.

River closed their eyes and pressed their face to the cage where Scream and Dream sat, tails intertwined. River knew without opening their eyes that Scream would be looking around her, wild-eyed, and Dream would have his eyes half closed, copacetic as ever. They let the purrs calm them for a minute, then re-entered the world.

"Thank you all so much for stopping by to help," they said, aggressively cheery. "Jack, you can go get me a coffee with milk and sugar. Simon, please break down and stack the boxes on the back wall. Grandma Jean ..."

Simon's grandmother looked up from the bag of cookies she was offering Cassidy.

"Please let her keep giving me cookies," Cassidy requested.

"Grandma Jean, keep giving Simon cookies."

"I will," she said, making it clear that she would have anyway. "You don't look well at all, dear," she said to Cassidy.

She had to stand on her tiptoes to do it, but she put her palm on Cassidy's forehead, checking for a fever.

"Maybe just the cookies," Simon said quietly.

"Got any sweetness left for me?" Jean's boyfriend Clive asked as he approached, waggling his eyebrows.

"Surprised you can take much more sweetness after this morning," Jean said, leaning into him. She turned to the rest of them and arched an eyebrow.

Simon's expression said, *I regret everything.*

"No need to be such squares," she sniffed. "Older people aren't post-sexual, you know. Come on, Clive. Let's go sit in Santa's lap."

They left, hand in hand, disappearing into the crowd.

"Wow," Cassidy said.

"God *dammit*, Grandma."

"What's *post-sexual*?" Gus asked.

"You know," Charlie mused, examining the shelter's booth, "If I built a little extension to this table, you could—"

"*Stop!*"

River hadn't meant to yell, but now that they had everyone's attention, they used it.

"Jack, where's my coffee? Simon ... go with him. Gus, go take a picture of the three weirdest things you can find here and then come back and show me."

"When you say *weird*—"

"Construe *weird* however it suits you. Adam and Wes, you should go with her. There's, like, a *lot* that she will find weird and offend people about."

Both Adam and Wes nodded instantly and took off after her.

That left only Charlie, who turned back to Cassidy.

"I haven't seen Dave in a while," he said.

Sometimes River amused themself thinking that if you looked up hardware store owner in the dictionary the picture would be of Charlie.

"I think he's doing well," Cassidy replied. "Dave's a good guy."

Charlie nodded. "He is."

"Mommy, that cat looks weird."

A little girl was pointing at the cage where Scream and Dream were now twined around one another. Her mother made a face.

"Cats are filthy and they make the house smell like pee. Let's go find a wreath," was her mother's response.

"Did you hear that?" River cooed to Scream and Dream. "You're filthy and you smell like pee."

Dream yawned. Scream continued to look like an Edvard Munch composition come to life. So, things were back to normal.

At noon, River had the cats who'd allow it dressed in their sweaters. They'd had the idea to enter the cats into the ugly sweater contest as a way to raise awareness of their availability for adoption the night before at Peach's while hanging out with Simon and scrambled to make them when they got home, manic from the sugar of five rounds of pie.

Cassidy had largely ignored River since the whole friend ambush that morning, about which River was relieved and disappointed. They'd left Charlie in charge of the booth as he was the one person River knew would neither embarrass them to Cassidy nor let any of the other cats escape.

Unfortunately, since the cats couldn't promenade to display their sweaters on their own, River had resigned themself to carrying them, which was how they came to be standing in front of hundreds of people and holding up a snarly Scream, who was twisting in River's arms to escape them and the red and green felt sweater that said *CATMAS* across the back with jingling bells all over it.

Didn't think that one through, River thought as the tintinnabulation echoed through their head.

They didn't win, though the crowd *Ooh*ed and *Aww*ed over the cats, as hoped.

"That's The Dirt Road Cat Shelter, which has cats to adopt over in aisle C, everyone!" the announcer read off her index card.

River hurried to get back to the booth only to find it already swamped. Charlie and Rye were both showing people cats.

A couple who looked just married held up Muffuletta, a large white cat that liked to sun himself on his back next to the window. River would slide their hand up and down his stomach and chest as he purred with his eyes closed.

A little boy with thick glasses was hugging Buffalo, the calico cat whose orange and black fur resembled buffalo plaid. Her whiskers brushed his cheek and he giggled. Buffalo licked his nose.

"Oh, look at his little sweater!" a woman cooed, pulling a man who could've been her husband or her brother over to River. "Is he up for adoption?"

River stroked Scream's little face and nodded, holding her up to the woman.

"Her name's Scream," they said hoarsely.

"Oh he's adorable!" the woman said, snuggling Scream. "We've gotta have him."

River found a smile and nodded, reaching for the paperwork and trying to hold back tears.

CHAPTER 12

Cassidy

When the doors closed on the final day of Craftmas and the music cut out, leaving only the dim hum of voices and lights, Cassidy put a hand to his head to make sure no bloody shards of skull were poking out his eye sockets. It was always a shock that pain so extreme could leave no visible trace.

He'd expected to feel relief. After all, he and Nora had moved more merchandise this year than ever before, and gotten enough custom orders to see them through the winter. It was over and he could go home and sleep for a week if he wanted to.

But there was no room even for relief. He'd pushed his body past the point of sense and now it was out of his control. Flashes of color would pull his eyes until the space around them made a tunnel. Sounds would jar and morph back into nothingness as his brain tried to process them. He was in an echo chamber, trying to make his carcass do as he commanded it.

Arms: pick up that box. Legs: support weight. Stomach: do not heave.

Despite all this, though, Cassidy was hyper-aware of River. Even though his body was unable to process basic sounds and movements, it seemed to be tuned like a satellite dish to the booth beside his, where River was an open wound, pulsing with a very different kind of pain.

"A hundred percent success," Cassidy said.

"Huh? Oh. Yup." River eyed the empty cages like they had no clue what they were supposed to do with them.

"Do you need help getting those to your car?" Cassidy offered.

River raised wide eyes gleaming with tears and then fled.

Cassidy followed them to the door outside. It was dark and the parking lot was a slush of gray snow and cigarette butts. River was squatting on the ground, spine pressed into the brick wall of the building.

The cold air rushed through Cassidy's lungs, mercifully numbing him inside.

"Hey," Cassidy said softly.

River stood and turned away from Cassidy, wiping at their eyes and swearing.

"You gonna be okay?"

River nodded, then shrugged.

"Pretty stupid to work at a cat shelter if you don't want any of the cats to get adopted, huh," they said shakily.

Their long brown hair fell around their face and Cassidy wanted to stroke it back. To hold their face in his hands and say, *No, not stupid. Sweet. Caring. Sensitive.*

"Just," River said breathily, wrapping their arms around their torso. "They're my friends."

The words were almost stolen by the wind, but Cassidy made them out.

"I understand. I'm so sorry."

River laughed humorlessly. "Thanks. How did you do?"

"Good."

"Good." River nodded, then looked at Cassidy. "You look ... not good. I mean, you look good. You seem ... Jesus Christ."

"I'm not feeling my absolute best," Cassidy said mildly.

"What's that called again? Where you super understate something for the opposite effect. We learned about it in English class."

"I don't know, sorry."

"Thanks for checking on me," River said. "Looks like you should go home and get some rest. I hope you feel better."

"Thanks," Cassidy said. And then, before he had a chance to question or second guess it, he said, "Would you want to have dinner with me this weekend?"

River blinked once, twice, then cocked their head. If Cassidy had been in better shape, he might have had a prayer of following their nonverbals, but as it stood, he could only stand there, waiting for grace or dismissal.

"Yes?" River finally said.

"Good?" Cassidy asked.

"I mean, yes. I would. Dinner. With you."

River rolled their eyes at themself.

"Saturday night?" Cassidy asked.

River nodded, eyes huge.

"I'll text you," Cassidy said. Then he managed, "Bye, River," before bolting around the corner to throw up, blessedly out of sight.

CHAPTER 13

River

"Okay, let's see what we're working with," Adam said, standing in front of River's small closet in their room above the cat shelter.

River had texted an SOS to Adam after spending days trying on every combination of clothing they had and finding absolutely nothing they could possibly wear to dinner with Cassidy Darling.

Gus had come along to lend her sartorial eye because, as she put it, "Daddy only wears graph paper shirts and boring beige pants. Why is *he* helping you?"

"Ugh, I have nothing to work with," River groaned and fell onto their bed, twisting at the last moment to avoid landing on Croissant, the tabby who had quietly curled up in a perfect circle in the direct center of the bed while they weren't looking.

Adam hummed tunelessly as he flipped through River's clothes.

"Oh, River. I gotta show you my weird things," Gus said, perching on the side of the bed. "Daddy wouldn't let me come back to your booth on Sunday."

River sent Adam a silent *Thank you*.

"Yeah, show me," they said, curious to see what Gus considered an oddity at Craftmas.

Gus held out her hand to Adam, who passed her his phone. In the last two years, Gus had become fascinated by photography and started an Instagram account where she posted images of bugs, lizards, and whatever other creatures appealed to her. Since she was too young for a phone of her own, she nabbed Adam or Wes' whenever she could, often leaving Adam's camera roll full of spiders, which terrified him.

"Okay, so!" Gus said with relish. "You know how Santa is, like, *not* real?"

"Uh, yeah?" River said hesitantly.

The last few years, it had been all Adam and Wes could do to keep Gus from running up to entire classrooms full of elementary school children and informing them all of this fact.

She held up Adam's phone to show River a picture of someone in a Santa costume smoking a joint outside the doors to the convention center.

River snorted. "Good lord."

They swiped to the next picture, which was a needlepoint stand that made stockings with sayings on them. The stocking in question said, *He died*.

"This is like they murdered a giant and then stole one of their socks," Gus said, giggling.

"I assume that's supposed to be ... about Jesus?" River ventured.

"Yeah," Gus said. "People are, like, *obsessed* with that guy."

The third picture was indecipherable at first, then Gus flipped it sideways. It was someone dressed like an elf, with a long streamer of toilet paper stuck to the bottom of their pointy green elf slipper.

"A triptych of Craftmas weirdness. Good job," River said, high-fiving her.

"Try this on for me." Adam handed them a pair of jeans and a sweater that they would never wear together.

They changed in the bathroom and came out frowning at their reflection.

"You look great!" Adam said. "How do you feel?"

"Um."

"No, no." Gus dismissed. "This isn't a River outfit. It's all ..." She waved her hands around to indicate general wrongness. "It's only boy stuff."

"Honey, remember we've talked about how clothes don't have genders. Anyone can wear anything they want."

"Yeah, I know that. But these are not right for River."

Ruling delivered, she splayed her hand gently on Croissant's sleeping back and patted her softly.

River deeply appreciated Adam's sincere attempts to uncouple clothes from gender, but Gus got River's gender intuitively, as only a kid who hadn't yet been fully indoctrinated into a society hamstrung by binaries could.

"She's right," River said.

"Hmm." Adam went back to the closet's meager offerings.

Gus squinted at River's outfit, then went to stand beside Adam. Side by side, they were a matched set. Both of their blond heads canted slightly to the right, both of their right hands were in their back pockets, and both of them held their weight in their right hips. River took a sneaky picture.

Gus pulled out a pair of bleached jeans, a long red T-shirt, and River's favorite oversized gray grandpa cardigan and handed them the outfit.

"Fashion show!" she crowed.

This was better. The outfit was more them, for sure. But there was something that still wasn't right.

"You look great!" Adam said when they emerged from the bathroom.

Gus gazed at them critically.

"I don't think the red."

"Yeah," River agreed. "Too much for a first date."

"What?" Adam looked from one of them to the other. "Why?"

"Oh, Daddy," Gus said. "You don't get it."

River bit their lip to keep from laughing at the look on Adam's face.

"This is better," she said, handing River a bias-cut long T-shirt dyed in shades of purple and black. "Oh and where's that necklace with the moons?"

River dressed as Gus instructed. When they came out of the bathroom, she had shoes ready: their white Doc Martens.

River looked in the mirror. They'd tried on something similar and decided it looked too sloppy; not date-worthy enough. But Gus was right. This was them. She put the necklace over their head and nodded once, satisfied.

"Do that messy gray makeup thing you do sometimes."

River nodded, feeling better by the minute. Thank god Gus had come along.

"You might have the makings of a personal stylist yet," they said.

Gus wrinkled her nose. "No way. I'm a scientist and I'm gonna invent things that will make the world way better."

"Well, you just invented an outfit that's making the world better for me today."

Gus cocked her head, considering this reframe.

"Nah," she concluded. "Clothes are not important."

Despite Gus' conviction, clothes *were* important to River. Wearing a garment that didn't feel right—that didn't feel in line with how River felt—could ruin their whole day.

And they couldn't always tell as soon as they donned an article of clothing that it would affect them this way. Sometimes an outfit would look fine when they left the house. Then, they'd catch a glimpse in a shop window or a rearview mirror and hate the way it looked on them. The way it made them look. What it exaggerated, what it diminished, and how those changes made them feel.

On the other hand, the euphoria of catching a glimpse of the way something hung or clung that was positive could invest that garment with the power to make their whole day—hell, sometimes their week. It was unpredictable and impermanent, but it was what River was always chasing.

River snapped a selfie and sent it to their friend Mikal.

These boots or black sneakers?

Their phone lit up with a FaceTime right away.

"Lemme see the sneakers," Mikal said.

River held them up.

"Boots," they said. "What's the makeup situation?"

"I was gonna do the smoky gray shadow?"

"That looks great on you. Hair?"

"I don't know. Down?"

Mikal narrowed their eyes, examining River.

"If you leave it alone, great. But if you'll play with it the whole time, or if it's gonna be in your face, maybe put it up."

"I probably will play with it and it will be in my face, but ... I like it cuz it softens my jaw a little."

"Okay, problem solved, you're welcome."

"Ha, you didn't do anything."

"Psh, we both know the shoes were a gambit to talk about how you're feeling about your date."

River rolled their eyes, but Mikal was right, damn them. They'd only met a month before, online, but although Mikal had been born and raised in Philadelphia and River in rural Wyoming, they'd become close quickly, bonding over a deep understanding of the difficulties of being nonbinary in an environment that didn't recognize them as such at first glance.

"I'm super nervous," River admitted.

They'd already filled Mikal in on the circumstances. Mikal found the entire thing hilarious, from the taxidermy to the holiday craft fair to the ask-out-while-seriously-ill. "It's like something from a fucked up, gay Hallmark movie!" they'd laughed.

"I don't even know where we're going—he only said dinner and ..."

"You like to prepare for these things. I get it."

"Yeah, well. I get anxious that I'll dress wrong, or order the wrong thing, or ..."

"Well, dinner dates are kinda the worst when it comes to thinking there are right and wrong ways to act. They're so, like, traditional."

"Yeah. And I ... You know, I had that *thing* last fall and it threw me."

The *thing* in question was a relationship—if you could call a string of four dates, some bad sex, and an awkward mutual backing away a relationship. River chose not to.

"Sure, because that dude wasn't trans competent and didn't bother educating himself with even so much as a google search, so clearly he didn't give a shit. Besides, he was an Aries. I can't."

River chuckled.

"I don't know that Cassidy is competent either," they admitted. "I mean, he didn't misgender me, so that's something."

"The barest of bare minimums, but better than nothing. What's the worst-case scenario here?"

"That he's also an Aries?"

Mikal grinned.

"Okay, I guess the worst-case scenario is like he freaks and murders me."

"You're being infuriatingly literal today."

"You're the one who said *worst*."

"Yeah, that's what being literal means."

River chewed on their lower lip and looked out the window.

"Um. That he'll like me. And I'll really like him cuz I think he likes *me*. But it'll turn out he likes who he *thinks* I am instead of the real me, and wants me to be ..."

"A dude."

"Yeah. And it's hard to explain to him or be sure of myself because sometimes that feels okay ... well, close to okay."

"You deserve better than close to okay, River."

"Well, yeah, okay, when you put it like that," they grumbled.

Mikal got that look on their face that meant they were being serious now so you better not mess around.

"Do *not* go into this jawn ready to settle for someone else deciding who you are. That's bullshit and a recipe for dissatisfaction. Believe me."

And River did believe them, because Mikal had told them the story of their ex-boyfriend whom they'd adored. Until they came out as non-binary, and their ex had said he supported Mikal, but didn't change the way he treated them and when Mikal expressed dissatisfaction made it clear that he had not, in fact, been supportive so much as clueless.

"How can I *know*, though?" River asked. "Like, on the apps, I can be specific about things so it's clear from the beginning. Who I am, what I'm into. But Cassidy and I ..."

"You met the old-fashioned way, when he brought you the almost corpse of a cat."

"Ha. Yes."

"You know, there's one crystal clear way you can know what his relationship to transness is."

"There is?" The knot in River's stomach loosened a bit. Mikal always knew what to do. "What?"

"You ask him," they said gently.

River slumped, deflated.

"I know, I know, it violates the River Mills protocol. But it's better than guess work."

"Ugh."

"Well, if you want, you can wait until you're already super into him, still don't know what he wants or expects from you, and then roll the dice on heartbreak."

"Oh, good, a better answer."

"Listen, if there were some surefire way to suss it out, I'd be the first to tell you. But you could have a whole dinner date, and if you don't bring it up, you'll be just as unsure as you are now."

"I don't even know how to ask that!" River exclaimed. "It's not like I want to be in the dark. Ugh, it's so unfair. Cis straight people don't have to do this shit."

"Yeah, but they have to be in cis straight relationships. That can be punishment enough," Mikal said, looking as if they smelled something unsavory. "Listen. Are you listening?"

"Oh my god, you're so dramatic. Yes, I'm listening. How could I not be."

"Good. So. I'd like to introduce you to a radical concept—all credit to my therapist, shout out to Margot; I love you, girl. But not in a transference way. It blew my mind; may it blow yours."

"Pray, blow me."

Mikal grinned. "Consider the radical notion that this date is about *you*. To see how *you* feel about *him*. It's up to him to impress you, not the other way around. That means you should be yourself. You should ask him whatever you want to know. And you should worry about forming an opinion about him, not about if you're making him like you."

I hate when things are about me.

"At every point," Mikal went on, "ask yourself how you feel in response to what he says or does. Do you like it, hate it, feel weird about it, whatever. If you're yourself, you stand the best chance of evaluating his responses to you usefully."

Wait, wait. That made sense. A horrible kind of sense that, at the moment of it sinking in, cast into relief all the other dates River had been on. Dates where they had worried the entire time how they were coming off, how they were being perceived, how this expression or that story landed with the other person. Dates where they'd focused so much on making the best impression they could —because who wouldn't want to put their best foot forward?— that it never occurred to them that dating could be anything other than trying to win. Win their date's good opinion, attention, attraction, respect.

"Oh dear god," River said.

"Yeah. I know. Therapy, I'm telling you."

CHAPTER 14

River

When Cassidy arrived, River was in the cats' playroom standing awkwardly in the corner to avoid getting cat hair all over their clothes before dinner.

"What are your intentions toward River?" River heard Rye ask from the front desk.

River recognized their seriousness as faux, but Cassidy responded nonetheless. "My intentions are to take them out to dinner and get to know them."

"All right, well, have them home by eleven," Rye said.

"Hey," River said. "He's kidding. About the curfew. And your intentions."

"Curfew, yes; intentions, no," Rye said.

"Intentions don't always count for shit anyway," River said.

"Wow," Cassidy said, eyes only for River now. "You look great."

Cassidy also looked great. He wore well-fitting dark jeans, black ankle boots, a forest green button-down shirt, and a vest in a gorgeous plaid of blue and green against a field of fine gray wool.

"You do too," River managed. It was a miracle they were able to speak at all, given the size of the nervous lump in their throat.

"Bye, Riv, have fun," Rye called after them. River turned and gave him a warm smile of thanks. Rye winked.

Cassidy had a large truck, and like all vehicles in Wyoming in the winter, its lower half was spattered with a combination of mud, snow, and salt that River was careful not to smear all over themself while getting in.

They sat, hands in their lap, seatbelt safely buckled, desperately trying to control anything they could while the rest of the world spiraled into uncertainty.

Be yourself, be yourself, they repeated like a mantra, in an attempt to keep scarier repetitive phrases out of their head.

"River?"

"What's that?" River asked, becoming aware that Cassidy was talking to them.

"I said, is Martelli's good for you? Or we could go to the Chop House instead. Whichever you'd prefer. I didn't make a reservation because, well, Garnet Run."

You could walk into any restaurant in the area at eight on a Saturday night and never have to wait to be seated.

Be yourself, be yourself, be yourself.

"Actually, could we do something else?" They blurted it out so they couldn't lose their nerve. "Dinner is so formal and I get nervous and it's all like 'What do you do?' 'And what do *you* do?' and there's so much pressure."

They'd delivered this blurt out the windshield of Cassidy's truck, to the darkness of the parking lot, and now they forced themself to look at Cassidy.

He was frowning, but nodded.

"Of course. We can do whatever you want. The only thing is ..."

Cassidy's stomach, at that moment, let out a growl that might've been audible in places that required dinner reservations.

"Uh, that says it all, I suppose," he said, sheepishly putting a hand on his stomach.

River felt awful.

"Oh, no, we can go to dinner," they insisted. "Sorry, I didn't think of the whole hunger thing. Martelli's sounds good."

Turns out, they imagined themself saying to Mikal when asked for a rundown of their date, *that people go to dinner because of this pesky human drive called* hunger *as well as to get to know one another in the antiquated ritual of dating.*

Cassidy narrowed their eyes and River had the distinct sense that they were being solved like a math problem. They squirmed in the awkwardness they'd created.

"What if we go get some snacks and have them in the truck on the way to wherever?" he suggested.

He didn't sound put out or irritated.

"Yes, great. Okay."

Cassidy started the truck and navigated down the long, dark road away from the shelter.

"Oh! I have an idea of where we can go," Cassidy said, tapping a rhythm out on the steering wheel with one hand as he steered with the other. He was smiling to himself.

"Where?"

"I think maybe I'll keep it a surprise," Cassidy said.

Oh, great, surprises, my favorite thing. I love not being able to prepare myself for what's coming and what will be expected of me there.

But having already asked for one change of plans, River didn't feel they could ask for another, so they leaned back and let Cassidy ferry them where he would.

"Oh no, it's closed!"

Cassidy had brought them to Circles, an ice-skating rink that had been the backdrop to many birthday parties in River's childhood, as well as a Prom afterparty that they'd excused themself from for the same reasons they'd eschewed Prom itself. They hadn't been in years but they could conjure the particular smell of popcorn, bleach, and ozone that hung in the air strong enough to pervade their clothes for hours after visiting.

The handwritten sign on the door beneath the CLOSED said *Gone Fishing*. River assumed it was a joke, but you never knew.

Cassidy looked deflated. He'd hinted at a combination of foods that they wanted to procure for their date, but Smith's had been out of two things he needed. Now his improvisational date idea had let him down as well.

"God, I'm sorry, River. I really wanted to show you a good time. I should've planned better."

He slumped against the truck.

"Hey, no. Cassidy, I'm the one who asked to change your plans. I should've just done what you wanted."

They stood beside Cassidy's truck, shivering. Cassidy grabbed them by the shoulders, and River started. But Cassidy was looking into their eyes intently.

"I didn't care that it be dinner," he said. "I wanted to get to know you. Not drag you to the grocery store and an abandoned building."

Could it be that *Cassidy* was as nervous as River? That Cassidy wanted to impress them?

Um, duuuuuh, if he's worth anything! River heard Mikal's voice saying.

"I want to get to know you too," River said. "Actually, I know a place we could skate. Well, in our shoes."

Cassidy's eyes lit up.

"Great!"

He handed River the keys to the truck and got into the passenger seat.

"Oh, sorry, do you drive?" he asked.

River slid into the driver's seat.

"I do. But are you sure you want me to drive your car? Truck, I mean."

"Sure." Cassidy shrugged. "Easier if you know where we're going. I'm bad with directions."

Unsure, River turned the key in the ignition. That made sense, kind of.

River drove with the care of someone who wouldn't be able to pay for any damage they inflicted, which meant they didn't talk much until they pulled into the parking lot of their old school.

"It's behind that copse of trees."

Cassidy grinned, then took off through the snow in their nice leather ankle boots like a big kid.

"Oh, I see it!"

Cassidy's voice drifted back as they quickly outpaced River. Running in snow was even worse than running in not snow, and they approached at a walk.

Cody Lake had frozen over by the middle of November since River was a kid, except for the last two years. As climate change wreaked havoc globally, a delay of two weeks had been added to the lake's freeze date.

Cassidy reached the ice.

"Hey, wait!" River yelled, but Cassidy didn't seem to hear.

They ran, then, heart screaming with instant fear. They grabbed Cassidy by the arm when he was five steps out onto the ice and dragged him back to shore.

"It's might not be safe," River gasped.

Cassidy's eyes were wide.

"You gotta test it."

"Okay." Cassidy looked sheepish. "Of course. Thanks."

"Fuck, you scared me," River said, blowing out the anxiety and bending over at the waist, relief flooding through them.

"Sorry, I, uh. I just got scared."

I t had been the weekend after Thanksgiving, and all River had wanted to do was follow Adam and Marina as far from the house as they could get. Their father had gone hunting with a buddy and tried to take Adam with them. When Adam had demurred, their father had turned to River.

Seven was the age he'd begun hunting with his own father and brothers, he'd said. River should join them.

The panic that the invitation catalyzed was an unconscious, gut-deep one, that prompted River to run after Marina when she left the house, caring nothing for what they were running toward, so long as they were running away from the kill.

Adam had veered off somewhere, but River had followed his sister to the edge of the pond. She stood, looking out over the ice, smoking a cigarette and sipping from a metal flask shaped like a smiley face. River imagined that the liquid inside the smile would taste like the sparkling apple juice their mom served at holidays. Her cheeks were flushed.

"You know, he's never gonna stop," she said without turning around.

"Stop what?" River asked.

They didn't have to ask who she meant. *He* was always their father.

"You know. Being how he is. To you. To all of us."

"I don't like him," they confessed.

When Marina talked to them, it was a treat. They always tried to keep the conversation going as long as possible. Usually that wasn't very long. River could never figure out what they said wrong to make her silence, though.

Marina snorted, smoke blowing from her nostrils like a bull.

"Yeah, no shit. No one likes him."

"Larry likes him," River said.

After all, why would he go hunting with their father if he didn't like him.

"Larry," Marina declared, "is a piece of shit."

"Oh."

She stabbed her cigarette out on the bottom of her boot and put it in her pocket. "You shouldn't listen to him," she said, stepping out onto the icy edge of the pond. "Whatever he says—*whatever*—you don't listen. Understand?"

River did not understand. You *had* to listen to your parents, didn't you?

Marina took another step.

"I'll get in trouble."

"You have to be careful," Marina said. Behind her back, River crept closer. "You can't count on the ice to hold you. The edges might be solid, but the middle can still give way."

"How can you tell?"

"You know, getting in trouble with someone who's wrong isn't the same thing as being wrong yourself."

River tried to make a connection between the ice and their father and being wrong, but couldn't see how the pieces went together.

Marina crouched and knocked on the ice as if someone might answer. Might open a door for her beneath it and welcome her to another world.

She sipped from her flask and lit another cigarette. When she turned around River saw tears glistening in her eyes.

"Get a rock. The heaviest you can find. If you can throw that out on the ice and it doesn't crack, it's probably safe."

Something was wrong, but River didn't know what it was. And when they didn't know what to do, they did what they were told. They found a rock, the heaviest they could lift, and brought it to the edge of the pond.

"Go ahead. Throw it."

River threw the rock. It didn't go far; only about as far as Marina was out on the ice. It thudded with a muffled *crrch*.

Marina let out a breath, then started to laugh.

"Guess it's safe," she said, voice strange and tight. "Come on out."

River stepped carefully onto the gleaming surface. Beneath the treads of their snow boots, the ridges and whorls of the ice felt like scar tissue, a texture you could read like history.

Marina grabbed them by the jacket and pulled them close. She slung her arm around their shoulders.

"Sorry you were born into this shit family," she'd said, her words rolling together into a sustained melody. "Get out any way you can."

" **R**iver?"
 Cassidy had a hand on their shoulder and was peering at them intently.

River surfaced.

"Are you okay? What happened? You feeling all right? Can I do something?"

Snow seeped through the knees of the jeans River had chosen so carefully for their date.

They looked up at the night sky. Stars winked in the velvet darkness, high above the trees and the ice and the man who was crouching next to them, eyes full of empathy.

S omething was wrong. Cassidy had enjoyed River's concern until he realized it was panic. River had stared blankly at the ice, eyes gone far away.

"Hey," Cassidy said softly. "Let's go back to the truck. It's pretty cold out here."

"You wanted to skate," they said flatly.

"I'm good. How about we have some snacks?"

River nodded and dragged themself up.

"Sorry," they said miserably. "I was thinking about my sister."

Cassidy slid into the driver's seat and turned the key one click to get some heat. His mind was racing, gathering all the bits of information he'd just witnessed and attempting to piece them together.

"We should have just gone to dinner," River said flatly.

Cassidy opened the bag of kettle corn and held it out to them. They took a handful, ate it, and only then seemed to realize what they'd consumed.

"Damn. That stuff's good."

Cassidy smiled, relief calming his nervous system.

"Yeah, it's addictive," he agreed. "When I was little, every

Christmas my aunt and uncle would send us these huge tubs of popcorn. You know, the kind divided into three sections, with cheddar popcorn, buttered popcorn, and caramel corn? I would eat the caramel corn and the buttered popcorn together to get the sweet and savory in one bite. My brother and sister thought it was gross, but it's basically kettle corn."

"Family is so weird," River said, staring out the window. "Who decided that the way we're supposed to prove we love each other is by sending one another huge tubs of corn?"

"I don't know. Probably catalogs."

"Catalogs were like online shopping before online shopping existed, huh?" River said.

Cassidy flipped them off good-naturedly.

"Hey, I'm not *that* much older than you."

"I dunno," River shrugged. "You're pretty old."

Cassidy was thirty to River's twenty-one.

"Does it bother you that I'm older?" he asked.

"Huh? No," River said, like it had never occurred to them.

"I wonder if you can still get those tubs of popcorn."

"We could anonymously send tubs of popcorn to everyone we know," River said. "Hmm, now I'm rethinking; popcorn is a great gift."

"Well, you just solved all my holiday gift list problems."

"What, you didn't lovingly pick out handmade gifts for all your dearly beloveds at Craftmas?" River joked.

"Yeah, in all my free time, when I wasn't in my booth, rescuing cats from the tops of trees, or puking my guts out," Cassidy said.

River grinned. "Did you know you were on the news? Shirtless."

Cassidy groaned and nodded.

"Yeah, you're the like seventh person to inform me of that. A lady at the gas station asked if she could set me up with her daughter yesterday."

"Well, you're an eligible bachelor; what do you expect?"

"Ha, I don't know what I'm eligible for, and bachelor sounds like something out of Jane Austen, but I guess I'll take it."

River ripped open the bag of spice drops and popped some in their mouth. They made a face.

"These are so weird. My friend Nate used to eat them in the car driving home from school every day. They're, like, gross, but then good, and then gross. But the suspense is just enough to keep me going. Hmm."

They ate some more.

"So, speaking of puking your guts out, how long did it take you to feel better after Craftmas?" River asked. "You seemed pretty rough."

"Yeah. It's worse when it's long periods of time. And it's worst when it's long periods of time in a row. So Craftmas was the worst-case scenario. Usually, when it's just the grocery store or something I can get in and out quick enough that I'm only semi-zapped."

Cassidy realized his mistake as soon as it was out of his mouth, but there was nothing he could do. Maybe River wouldn't notice.

"Wait, but we went into the grocery store to get the food."

Damn it.

"So are you zapped now?"

River's eyes were narrowed accusingly.

"Semi-zapped," Cassidy admitted reluctantly.

"Cassidy!"

River elbowed him. It wasn't hard enough to hurt, but felt intimate, like River presumed rights over his body. Cassidy shivered, surprised by how much that prospect appealed to him.

"You should've let me go in and get the food," River protested.

"What kind of a date would it be if I sat in the truck and you went grocery shopping?"

"Um, a better one than if we both go grocery shopping and you end up feeling like shit!"

River looked angry.

"I don't feel like shit. I'm happy to be here with you."

Cassidy meant it. Well, the second part, anyway.

"So, you're saying that you'd rather suffer than inconvenience me?"

"Well."

"Just FYI? It's not inconvenient for me to go get something in a store so that you aren't physically sickened."

Cassidy got the distinct sense that River had edited a *you idiot* from the end of that remark.

"Noted," Cassidy said.

They sat in silence that wasn't exactly awkward for a moment. Then River's expression turned impish.

"You wanna do something funny?"

River pushed the shopping cart toward the truck with a grin. They had found the huge tubs of popcorn at the third store they'd gone to, four of the metal tubs rattling in the cart, each one in a different garish Christmas print. River had refused to let Cassidy accompany them into any of the stores, dismissing his offers with a scowl.

"Got 'em!"

"Yes!" Cassidy crowed. "Now what's our plan?"

River's plan, it turned out, was to leave a tub of popcorn on the front step of four people's houses anonymously and see what happened. They had bought four cards to write messages on, too.

"Whose houses?"

"Well, one at my brother's place, for sure. Then Rye and Charlie's place. It would be really funny to leave one at Adam's," they mused. "But you should pick people too. If you want?"

Cassidy was delighted. But more than he wanted to see what Nora would do if she found a bucket of that long-forgotten popcorn on her door, he wanted to watch River experience what their people would do. He wanted to share it with them.

"Let's start off with whoever you want and I'll give it some thought," Cassidy offered, loading the tubs into the truck.

River nodded, then pushed the cart to the cart return, despite abandoned ones littering the parking lot.

"Okay," they said. "Let's go."

CHAPTER 16

Cassidy

dam Mills' house glowed in the middle of Knockbridge Lane from what must've been hundreds of strands of fairy lights.

"Damn," Cassidy said. "That must've taken forever."

River smiled fondly.

"My niece wanted the most lights last Christmas, so Adam made it happen."

"That's really sweet."

Cassidy parked the truck in a dark pocket across the street, in front of a house that looked abandoned.

"Okay, should we put it on the porch and just leave it so they find it in the morning, or ring the bell and hide to see them come get it?"

They looked at each other and smiled.

"Hide," they said in unison.

When River smiled, lines appeared around their eyes that Cassidy instantly wanted to see as often as he could.

River grabbed the tin printed with reindeer, ornaments, and stars, and they both snuck around the truck and into Adam's front yard.

"Kinda hard to be sneaky in front of a spotlight," Cassidy muttered.

When they got to the front stoop, an image dropped into Cassidy's head: the popcorn tin housed a jack-in-the-box that would sproing horribly into action when someone opened the lid. He snorted at the thought, which made River shush him, then begin to giggle themself.

"Okay, I'll—"

The tin slid through River's mittened hands and landed on the porch with a cartoonishly loud and ringing clang.

River swore and Cassidy clapped a hand over his mouth to avoid laughing.

They both bolted for the bushes next to the front stoop at the same time, which resulted in a tangled collision of limbs, both human and plant, when they landed.

"Ouch, shit," River said, then dissolved into giggles.

When the front door opened, a young girl that Cassidy remembered from Craftmas stepped out onto the porch.

"River?" Gus said. "What are you doing in the bushes? Did you put this here? What is it?"

River shushed Cassidy again, like Gus might simply cease to notice them if they were quiet.

"I can see you," Gus said matter-of-factly. "And the animal murderer. I mean, carnivore. What's your name again? Sorry I called you a murderer. Daddy says murder is a specific thing only for humans and that human life is different than animal life. I don't think it is. I think we just think so cuz we're humans and we're making the rules. Probably cows don't think their lives are worth less than ours."

Cassidy was charmed by the kid. He stood up, brushing off his clothes where leaves and snow clung to him.

"I'm Cassidy Darling." He held out his hand and Gus shook it gravely. "Nice to officially meet you."

At *officially*, Gus glanced at the bushes where River still crouched, completely visible, Cassidy could see now, from the front door.

"Nice to meet you. Why are you in the bushes?" she asked River.

They stood, finally.

"Hey, Gus. No reason. Just ... checking something. Oh, gosh, what's that on your porch? It was there when we showed up."

Gus narrowed her eyes, picked up the tin and dropped it on the step, replicating the clang it had made before.

"Gus?" called a voice from inside.

Two men came to the door behind Gus. Adam, River's brother, was slim and short, like River, but had blond hair and a sunny, open smile. His partner, who had also been at Craftmas, was tall, with short, dark hair and an intense mien.

"Can I help you?" Adam asked politely. "Oh, hello. You're River's ..." He trailed off and caught sight of River. "Hey, Riv."

"Ugh, that was a total fail," River said, crossing to them. "Have some popcorn from Santa."

"Santa is not real," Gus said.

"Fine, it's not from Santa. It's from an anonymous admirer."

"What's anon mouse?" Gus asked.

"It means you don't know who the person is."

"But we do know. The person is River."

River opened their mouth, but before they could speak, Adam said, "please do not let the words *ding dong ditch* leave your mouth in front of my curious child."

"Wouldn't dream of it. Okay, anyway, bye guys, love you!"

They started to retreat to the truck.

"That outfit looks way better than Daddy's," Gus said. "You're lucky I was there."

River's cheeks flushed and they grabbed Cassidy's wrist and pulled him away.

River looked mortified and Cassidy was utterly charmed.

Once he was behind the wheel, Cassidy elbowed River gently.

"So you enlisted help in figuring out what to wear on our date, huh?"

"No, shut up."

"You wanted to make a good impression, huh?"

"Ugh, *no*. Well, I mean, of course; everyone wants to make a good impression."

You like me. You wanted to look good for our date because you like me.

"Of course," Cassidy allowed, smiling to himself.

He drove in silence for a few minutes. Finally, River sighed.

"Yes, fine. I asked for feedback on my outfit because you never know how you're coming off to people and I wanted to feel in control and like I was portraying myself the way I feel."

"Please don't be embarrassed. I'm just teasing. I love that you wanted to feel good." Then, weighing the pros and cons, he admitted, "My sister told me what to wear and I just did it."

River finally looked at him.

"What were you going to wear?"

"Oh, I hadn't gotten that far. I was trying to decide if I should shave my beard."

River looked horrified.

"What? No! Why would you do that?"

Warmth glowed in Cassidy's chest.

"You like my beard?"

River nodded.

"I like everything about how you look. I mean ..."

They shook their head like they hadn't meant to admit this.

"I worried it might make me look ..." Cassidy frowned, not wanting to sound ignorant. "Um. I worried it might suggest that I'm masculine in a way you might not like," he settled on.

"Hmm." River cocked their head. "Can you explain more?"

Cassidy pulled the truck into a clearing beside the road.

"Want to lie in the truck bed and look at the stars?"

"Okay."

Cassidy pulled the wool blanket off the back of the seat and lowered the tailgate. They lay on their backs and looked up at a velvet dark thickly spangled with stars. Cassidy wished he knew the constellations well enough to point at the sky and whisper its organization into the shell of River's ear.

"Okay, so, please tell me if there are better ways to say what I'm thinking. I like my beard. But a lot of guys around here have beards and they're conservative, and they hunt, and they believe that masculinity means certain, fixed things. I don't share any of those qualities, so I worried that maybe you'd see my beard and think I did. Does that make sense?"

Cassidy's heart pounded. He desperately didn't want to say the wrong thing and offend River or seem ignorant or foolish.

River was staring intently at the stars, the slight wrinkle of a frown between their brows. They nodded.

"Yeah, it makes perfect sense. That's how the signifiers of gender go, often. You like something—a hairstyle, a color, a garment—for aesthetic reasons, but that thing is tied to other people's assumptions along binary gender lines. So your own aesthetics are under this pressure from a bigger cultural narrative. And you can't control the perception that someone is gonna have of that thing, only know that they're perceiving you and try and take ownership of those signifiers. But you never really know how big the chasm is between your aesthetic investment in that haircut or outfit and how each person perceives it."

Cassidy's head was spinning.

"So, uh. I guess you've thought about this before."

"Big time. That's why I asked my brother for help with an outfit. I, um. I wanted to look nice for our date, but wanted to look nice in the way *I* like. And I wasn't sure how it would be perceived. Turns out Gus was more of a help than Adam was."

"Well, you look really nice. I love the way you dress."

River looked at them.

"You do?"

Cassidy nodded.

"Yeah, it's ... flowy?" He looked at River more closely, wanting to find the words to properly honor their style. "Kind of in different proportions to more traditional clothes?"

River's smile was instant and radiant and Cassidy felt it in his guts.

"Do you want to know a secret?" he asked.

"Yes."

"Well, I don't wanna oversell it. I guess it's not really a secret." He was stalling. "I'm nervous that I'm gonna mess up and offend you in some way I probably won't even understand. And I don't want to mess up."

"Mess up how?"

"I don't even know how to explain it, exactly."

River sat up. "Or maybe you don't know how to explain it without potentially offending me?"

"Yeah maybe that too," Cassidy admitted.

"Maybe you could just say it however and we can talk about if there's a better way to say it after I understand?" River asked.

"Okay." Cassidy sat facing them, tugging the wool blanket over them both. "Um. I know you use they/them pronouns. But I'm not entirely sure what that means for you. And I want to be respectful but also I don't want to ignore your gender because I'm not exactly sure what it is. So ... yeah."

He held his breath, anxiously awaiting River's judgment.

"It's perfectly okay to ask people their pronouns or how they identify, Cassidy. It's not rude, if it's genuine. And it's much more respectful than making assumptions."

"Okay, cool. Then can you tell me more about ..."

"How I identify?" River prompted gently.

"Yeah. If you don't mind."

"I don't mind. This is a super normal conversation that trans and gender nonconforming people have *all* the time. It's only cis people who don't talk about it. Which is part of the problem, I think. Because not talking about something presumes that everyone agrees about how to describe or define it. But of course that's not true. You can take three women and ask what they think is feminine and get three different answers."

Cassidy nodded. Nora had said similar things in the past.

"People's convictions about what is feminine and what is masculine—and the notion that they're fixed, different things—is the root of so much transphobia. Kind of how misogyny is at the root of homophobia. 'Men acting like women,'" they said, accompanied by air quotes.

"Huh. I never thought about it like that."

Cassidy thought of the things that used to prompt boys in high school to call something *gay* or to label another boy as gay, and realized it was true.

"Yeah, cuz acting in ways that someone thinks of as feminine is only bad if you think being a woman is less valuable than being a man. If our society respected and admired women, then it wouldn't be an insult to be compared to one. So there's all this cultural stuff. But, to answer your question, I'm nonbinary. Social performances aside, when I think about how I feel when I'm alone? Sometimes I feel more toward the masculine side of things, sometimes more toward the feminine, sometimes pretty androgynous. Does that make sense?"

Cassidy nodded slowly, processing. "But you don't use different pronouns on different days?"

"No. Cuz even on days I feel more masculine, I don't feel completely male, et cetera. Like, if you think of the word nonbinary, it helps. I never feel on either side of a gender binary. I don't believe gender *is* a binary that's composed of either man or woman."

"Okay, I see. I think."

"It's maybe hard to understand if you've never thought analytically about your own gender. Like, I have friends who completely, straightforwardly, non-angstily *feel* like women or like men. And even if you feel like one gender or another, it doesn't mean that you *like* how people treat you. Then I have friends who have chafed against their birth sex their entire lives. And friends whose perception of their own gender has shifted over time. I have agender friends who don't feel like gender is a thing they have at all. There are so many ways to feel about your gender, and that's why it's great to ask. Really, when in doubt about anything, just ask."

"River?"

"Yeah?"

"Can I ask you something else?"

"Duh, I just said that."

"Can I kiss you?"

"That's not what I thought you were gonna ask," they said softly.

"I don't mean to interrupt our conversation. I'm really invested in it. But you did say when in doubt to ask." He shrugged. "I am in doubt. So I'm asking."

River's smile was slow and sweet.

"Yes, please."

Cassidy's heart began to race. He leaned in and cupped River's cheek in his palm. Their pupils were huge in the dark, their skin soft.

"I want to say that you look ... amazing right now, but I don't wanna use a word that seems gendered," Cassidy whispered.

"Thank you," River whispered back. "Let's table the linguistic discussion until it isn't totally ruining the moment."

Cassidy grinned.

"Noted."

He leaned in as River's eyes fluttered closed. When their lips met, River gasped and melted into the kiss. The sound sent liquid fire coursing through his veins. He deepened the kiss, River's mouth hot and soft, the taste of them exquisite.

River clutched Cassidy's shoulder and slid their other hand in his hair. They were trembling.

Cassidy ended the kiss and pressed his forehead against River's.

"Wow," River said, then looked embarrassed.

"I agree."

Cassidy took a moment to calm his breathing, then asked, "How are you doing?"

"Honestly? Freezing. And great."

They grinned and it slid through Cassidy like a sluice of heat.

Oh, damn. I am in so much trouble.

"Well, let's get you warm," he said.

But neither of them moved for a minute. They sat there, beneath a canopy of stars, and looked at one another.

So, so much trouble.

CHAPTER 17

River

Cassidy: *I had a wonderful time last night, River.*

River: *Me too*

Cassidy: *I really want to go out with you again.*

Cassidy: *What do you think?*

River: *Um, yes, I definitely want to*

Cassidy: *You just tell me where and what and I'm in.*

River: *You want me to plan it?*

Cassidy: *Well I did plan the last date and that didn't work out so well :D*

Cassidy: *I mean because we didn't end up doing what I planned, not because the date didn't work out well. The date worked out just excellently ;)*

Cassidy: *For me, anyway.*

Cassidy: *Shit, did I offend you? I can also plan the date?*

River: *Sorry, cat peed on me*

River: *The date worked out excellently for me too :)*

Cassidy: *Oh phew!*

River: *Are you free on thursday evening?*

Cassidy: *I'll be free whenever you want me.*

River: *It's a date :)*

"Why's it called that?" Gus asked, frowning at her math homework.

"No clue, dude. You're gonna outpace me in the math homework help department in a few years, sorry to say."

"You don't help me with my math homework," Gus said.

"I don't? What am I doing sitting here and working on your math homework with you, then?"

"Keeping me company," she said. "And sometimes I ask you questions so you don't get bored and leave."

River groaned.

"Jeez, the one way I thought I was useful to you," they joked.

"Don't be sad cuz *I* don't need you," Gus said. "Daddy says it's illegal for him to leave me alone in case I burn the house down or die or something, so he needs you cuz I don't want him to get in trouble."

River wished they were recording this to play for Adam later. They schooled their face to seriousness and nodded.

"That's considerate of you."

Satisfied that her consideration had been properly acknowledged, Gus went back to her math homework and River, freed from any need to assist her, picked up their phone and let their mind wander to Cassidy.

Cassidy, who'd been so flexible when they asked to change plans; who'd been kind and supportive when they got lost in that memory of Marina; who'd been fun and spontaneous and up for a prank.

Cassidy, whose kiss had been hot and sweet and gentle and promised so much more, if River wanted it.

Cassidy, who had asked them out on a second date.

"Are you trying to figure out where to take that guy in our bushes on a date?"

Heat rose in River's cheeks and they turned their phone over on the table so results of the search *Where to take someone on a second date* were no longer visible to Gus' prying eyes.

"Has your dad discussed nosiness with you yet?" River grumbled.

"Yes. He says it's not polite and can make people feel uncomfortable. But how do you know what questions will make someone uncomfortable? *I* wouldn't be uncomfortable if someone asked me a question. If I didn't wanna answer then I wouldn't."

River was swamped with the cocktail of feelings they often experienced when hanging out with Gus: intense relief that she was herself easily and without compromise and a guilty kind of envy that they were not.

"There's no good way to explain it or know for sure," River said. "But usually, if someone is doing something alone, like looking at their phone, then looking at it and commenting on it when they didn't ask you is considered rude."

"Oh. That's helpful."

She went back to her math book. Neon the cat ran into the kitchen in pursuit of something invisible to the human eye, and River went back to their phone.

All the suggestions for dates seemed to be for people in urban areas: art gallery tours and hot air balloon rides and being a tourist in your own city.

"Okay, but since I *did* see your phone, it's silly to pretend I didn't see it," Gus said. "Right? So can I ask?"

River smiled and put the phone away.

"Yeah, yeah, fine. I have a date with Cassidy on Thursday and I don't know what we should do."

"What exactly makes something a date?" Gus asked, eyeing the rules for factoring in her math book.

"There aren't rules. It could be anything. But you want it to be something special, I guess? Something you wouldn't do every day. And it's good if it's something that helps you get to know the other person."

"Can you give me an example?"

River could hear Adam's intonation whenever Gus said that—he'd swapped it in for her previous choice, *What are you talking about?*

"Yeah, like dinner and a movie is a classic date. Or going to a play or a concert."

"Dinner?" Gus said. "You have dinner every day. That's not special!"

"True. Dinner at a nice restaurant where you dress up, which you wouldn't always do."

"So going on a date is taking normal stuff and doing it fancier so you don't notice it's normal?" Gus asked.

"Uh, kind of, actually."

"Honestly, grown-ups are so stupid," Gus said dismissively. "Dinner is not fun. And watching a movie is what you do if you don't want to have to talk to someone."

"Okay, Gus, what would you want to do on a date?"

She shrugged. "Whatever I feel like doing. Then you *know* you're gonna have fun and you get to hang out with someone you like. Like when you keep me company while I do math."

River smiled. Grown-ups, they had to agree, really were quite stupid about some things.

CHAPTER 18

Cassidy

Dress comfortably and come over at 7?

That was all River's text had said, but of course Cassidy had agreed instantly.

When the doorbell rang a little before five, he'd just gotten out of the shower.

"'S open!" he called to Nora, pulling on sweats to go meet her in the kitchen. But instead of his sister's usual, 'Hi, honey, I'm home!' in the voice of a cheesy fifties' dad, the doorbell rang again.

"Get your ass in—" Cassidy said as he pulled the door open.

But it wasn't Nora. It was River, and they were crying and shaking with cold.

Cassidy's heart started pounding.

"River? What's wrong?"

"I th-think I k-killed them," they sobbed.

A thousand thoughts crash-landed in Cassidy's brain—worst case scenarios and unrelated hopes and the errant focus on a small beauty mark above River's left eyebrow.

"Why don't you come inside where it's warm and you can tell me what happened," Cassidy said, but River shook their head.

"I went out to get food for tonight and on the way back I, I, it just ... and I hit it."

The words tumbled out of River in a horrified slurry. They hung their head.

"Who?"

"A f-fox."

Cassidy took River in his arms as they wept, relieved that he didn't have to add harboring a fugitive to the list of hurdles in a new relationship. The cold of their coat said they'd been outside a while before ringing the doorbell.

"Oh, sweetheart."

He stroked River's hair back, and held them tightly. Slowly, their breathing slowed and steadied.

"Can you come look?" River asked hoarsely.

"Of course."

Cassidy tugged on his shoes and coat and followed River to their car. When they turned around, they held a fox cradled to their chest.

"I don't ..." They broke off, shaking their head, and held the fox out.

Cassidy was surprised by the magnitude of his desire to look River in the eye and tell them the animal was okay. Watch the sadness and guilt clear from their face and the sun come back in their eyes.

It broke his heart that he couldn't.

"I'm sorry," Cassidy said, and River dissolved into sobs.

It had begun to snow.

River had let themselves be led inside and out of their coat, and let Cassidy wrap a wool blanket that had been his mother's around their shoulders. They'd stopped crying; now their eyes were blank and inward-focused.

"Fuck, I can't believe I killed him." River said, raising tearful eyes to Cassidy. "I fucking ended his life forever. I'm death! For a whole neighborhood of foxes, I'm fucking *death*."

Cassidy bit the inside of his cheek to keep from smiling at how damn cute River was. He knew it was wrong to think that while they were so distressed, but everything about them made Cassidy want to hold them tight and soothe them.

He settled for rubbing River's blanket-draped shoulders.

"Don't be so hard on yourself," Cassidy said gently. "I get you're upset you killed her, but it was an accident."

River looked horrified.

"Oh god, I misgendered her! I murdered *and* misgendered her, I'm a monster."

Cassidy couldn't help laughing then. He pulled River into a hug.

"Can I tell you a secret?"

River frowned. "Is it actually a secret this time?"

"Huh?"

"Last time you said you were gonna tell me a secret and then it wasn't a secret."

"What did I say?"

"I don't remember," River said, throwing their arms wide. "It didn't end up being a secret!"

Cassidy wracked his brain.

"Yeah, no clue."

They sat there staring at each other. Tear tracks had dried tight on River's cheeks and their hair was a mess. Pink puffed the delicate skin of their eyelids and they'd bitten a tender spot in the center of their lower lip.

Now that Cassidy knew how River's lips felt against his own and it made him wonder if he'd taste the thinness of River's skin, how close the blood was to its surface in the spot they'd worried red.

"Um, I have ADHD," Cassidy said, wrenching his eyes away. "My memory is a little, uh, variable."

River nodded and leaned their head on his shoulder.

"So what's the secret this time?" they asked.

"Wait, what?"

River chuckled and scrubbed hands over their face.

"Where did you ...?"

"I put her in the freezer downstairs."

"Is that where you keep all your ..."

"Mhm. Just to give you a little time to think what you'd like done with her."

"Fuuuuck," River groaned.

"Oh, I remember what I was gonna say," Cassidy said brightly. "I was going to say that I have a lot of firsthand knowledge about this topic. And almost everyone who lives around here has hit an animal while driving. The longer you live in a rural place, the more likely it gets."

"I'll have to get Gus to calculate and explain the probability to me," they muttered.

"What's that?"

"Nothing, ignore me, sorry."

They dropped their head between their knees, blew out a harsh breath, and raked a hand through their hair.

Cassidy could practically feel the guilt and sadness coming off them and his heart hurt for River.

"Okay, you wanna know a *real* secret?" he offered.

River shrugged.

"You cannot tell a soul," Cassidy baited, pitching his voice low and gossipy.

River looked curious and annoyed about it.

"Fine, what?"

Gotcha.

"You know Mrs. Arkady?"

River wrinkled up their nose in thought. "The ancient librarian?"

"Yeah. She hit a lynx."

"Holy shit, seriously?"

"On my life, carried it in here in a bowling bag with her name stitched on it."

"God, she's like the size of a bowling bag herself," River said, wide-eyed.

"I'm just saying *I* wouldn't wanna mess with her," Cassidy said.

River smiled.

"It's always the quiet ones, huh?"

"You tell me," Cassidy said. "I've never been what you'd call quiet."

"Oh you should definitely watch out for us," River said. "Especially if you're a fox."

Cassidy laughed, then clapped a hand over his mouth.

"Too soon?" River asked.

"Never too soon to make yourself feel better," Cassidy said. "I've hit a deer, two squirrels, and a frog."

River winced.

"All accidents. The deer nearly killed me."

Cassidy shuddered at the memory. Only a moment, but a moment when he'd been sure he was about to die, then sweet relief slid through his bowels and the steering wheel stopped an inch from his sternum.

"But that's how I first got into taxidermy. I felt godawful that I'd killed them, and I wanted to honor the lives I'd accidentally taken away. That first squirrel, she was the one that set me on the path to where I am now."

"So you both impacted each other's lives," River murmured.

"Yeah, that's how I like to think about it." Cassidy stood. "Would you like to see?"

River rose slowly, keeping the blanket wrapped around their shoulders.

The glass cloche sat on a shelf beside the doorway down to the studio.

"This is Marge. I have no memory of why I started calling her Marge, I just did."

River peered at her intently.

"Hey, Marge."

"I'm much better than I was then," Cassidy felt compelled to say.

River was looking at the door and didn't respond.

"That where the fox is?" they asked finally.

"Yeah. Are you thinking about what you wanna do with her?"

"Do you think someone would want her?" River asked.

"Oh, definitely. Foxes are quite popular."

"You should have her, to ... Do you say, 'to taxidermy'? 'To stuff?'"

"I like how you always want to know the right words to use for stuff."

"Words are important."

"To mount," Cassidy said.

"Pardon?"

"The fox. You'd say that I'm going to mount her."

River snickered.

"Yeah, I know," Cassidy said, smiling. "The joke lost its effect after the first hundred times."

"I'll bet."

"Thank you," Cassidy said. "I'll honor her life as best I can. I promise."

"I know you will," River said, brushing away a tear that slid down their cheek.

They turned and rested their forehead against the door to the studio and whispered, "I'm sorry."

Cassidy's eyes got misty, too. Causing the end of a life was serious business, no matter how it happened.

"Phew, okay," River said, turning around and shaking their hands out. "Do you still wanna have our date?"

"So much," Cassidy admitted. "But if you'd rather reschedule I absolutely understand."

"I want to," River said. "I'm just afraid I might not be the best company tonight."

"Well, how about you don't worry about being good at anything or being company and just focus on doing whatever feels good to you. And I won't worry about trying to make you feel better and just focus on doing what feels good for me. What do you think?"

"Hmm." River narrowed their eyes. That sounded suspiciously like Mikal's suggestion. "I think you've been to therapy, and I'm very fucking relieved."

Cassidy laughed the laugh of someone whose therapist had indeed explained codependency to him.

"I did learn that in therapy and I'm gratified you appreciate it."

"That sounds good, then," River said. "After all, a fox gave its life so that we could have brie. Be a shame for it to go to waste."

"I'm a sucker for brie," Cassidy agreed. He was very willing to shift to a lighter tone. "We'd better do it."

"Hey, Cassidy?" River chewed on their lip. "Thanks."

CHAPTER 19

River

Cassidy's truck cut a path through the steadily falling snow and River followed in their car. As they drove, they called Rye, who answered with an enthusiastic "Hey, Riv! What's up?"

"Have you ever ... uh."

Rye shushed someone in the room.

"If it's awkward, illegal, embarrassing, or stupid, I've probably done it. What happened?"

"How would you handle showing up at someone's house sobbing because you hit a fox in the road and then having a complete meltdown over being a death bringer? Just, you know, hypothetically."

"Yeah, hypothetically, sure. How did said person respond to this alleged meltdown?"

"Like a total fucking sweetheart," River sighed.

They could picture Rye's wolfish grin.

"So, if you'd've asked me this five years ago, I would've said that no one is actually that sweet and you should cut and run because now that someone has seen you vulnerable they'll take advantage of you. *No,* I'm not telling them that! You entered mid-sentence!

Christ, Charlie, your particular brand of angel isn't common, but that's what I was *going* to say next."

River snickered.

"Anyway," Rye said. "Now I know, due to the *incredible* influence of my *amazing* partner—happy now?—that there really are people who are, like, bizarrely more kind than you might imagine if you grew up with people who weren't the best. Yeah, yeah, yeah," he added, and River heard him and Charlie kiss.

"Okay, he's gone," Rye said, tenderness lingering beneath his dismissal. "Anyway, Cassidy—I mean, this hypothetical person—might actually be another of the truly great humans that seem to be overrepresented in Garnet Run."

River picked at the rubber peeling off their gear shift.

"How would you change vibes if, say, you were segueing directly from sobbing in his arms to being on a date?"

"Just hypothetically?" Rye teased.

"Asshole. I shoulda called Simon."

"Oh, you should! Love that guy."

Rye and Simon were so different in demeanor that their friendship seemed odd at first, but Rye had a way of bringing out Simon's snarky side that River very much appreciated.

"Fine, I will then," River teased. "Bye."

"Wait, wait, okay, fine. Look, you're doing well cuz you had a freakout over a legitimately sad thing. And Cassidy, if he has any heart, will get that. We're done pretending it's not Cassidy, right?"

"Yeah."

"Good. So. You cried. You showed that you're a sensitive person who cares about animals. I'd imagine that would appeal to an ethical taxidermist and good human. So what's the real question, how to go from crying to fucking?"

River wouldn't have put it quite that way, but ...

"Well. Yeah."

"No problem at all: you just put it in the past and move on from here. If you're gonna end up dating, which you clearly are, then both of you will have to get to know all of each other's sides.

And sometimes that includes going from crying to fucking. Or fighting to fucking. Or fucking to crying. Or—"

"Okay, I get it, you're so bad at sex you make Charlie cry."

Come to think of it, maybe Rye brought out River's snarky side too.

"I am your *employer* so you're basically sexually harassing me right now."

"You should probably report me to HR so I can discipline myself."

"Noted. Seriously, though, Riv, it's gonna be fine. You move past it and embrace it. However you feel going forward, just act on that the same way you did when you showed up at his house. I'm sorry, by the way. I hit a raccoon last year and I felt fucking awful."

"According to Cassidy, everyone's hit something. Sucks."

"Here's what you do. Are you ready?"

River's hope soared. *Yes! Tell me the secret!*

"You just be yourself."

River groaned. "God dammit, why is everyone telling me that like it's a thing you can just *do*?!"

"I know, I'm disgusted with myself. It's the worst advice in the world and I'm so sorry to report that it's actually true. But you can only tell it's true after you've already done it. Sorry, kiddo, that's all I got."

"Okay, fine. Thanks," River grumbled.

"What?"

"I said thanks," River said.

"No, sorry, I was talking to—."

"River, it's Charlie."

River smiled. "Hey, Charlie."

"I was telling Rye to tell you that there's a big snowfall coming. Do you have everything you need? We have extra everything if you don't."

Bless Charlie, who always knew the weather and was always prepared enough for everyone.

"Thanks, Charlie. I'll be okay. I've got groceries and a lot of cat food." Then, realizing how that sounded, they amended, "For the cats, I mean. Not that I would run out of food and eat cat food. You get it."

"Good. Don't hesitate to call if you need anything. Or if the backup generator gives you any trouble. There's a tricky little ..."

While Charlie explained the details of how to reset the generator he'd installed, River took deep breaths through their nose and tried to feel like someone who was effortlessly themself. That probably required loving yourself, though, which River struggled with sometimes—especially when the self he was trying to love did things like sob uncontrollably in a date's arms.

"—jiggle it, okay?"

"Got it. Thanks, Charlie."

There was a pause and then Charlie cleared his throat.

"Forgive me for overhearing Rye's end of your conversation. I don't want to intrude, but, well. I had some trouble being, um, vulnerable. With Rye. About, erm, things."

"Sex!" Rye yelled.

"Yes, well. About things. Because I thought there were right ways to do things. Correct orders and timelines for things to happen. And Rye showed me that there aren't. There's only what works for the two of you." He cleared his throat. "You're a lovely, smart, kind person and Cassidy would be privileged if he gets to know you. That's all."

River smiled. When Charlie Matheson praised you, he meant it.

"Thanks, Charlie. I appreciate it."

A muffled *shworp* and then Rye's voice calling into the phone.

"And do *not* use those cats as an excuse not to fuc—"

"All right, bye, River. Don't hesitate to call if—"

"I need anything. Thanks. To both of you."

Then they hung up before Rye could give them any more advice.

❋

River had taken Gus' advice. They'd put together an evening of stuff that they would love to do themself, and hoped that maybe Cassidy's presence would enhance it.

A cheese plate with honey, fig jam, pistachios, sliced pear, and buttery crackers. Their current favorite indica-dominant hybrid. Comfort TV that you could attend to or not. And cats. Always cats.

"Wow," Cassidy said when they set the tray on the front desk.

"I usually hang out in the cat room, but there isn't a couch or anything, just some of those big pillows."

"I'm fine with the floor," Cassidy said.

His gaze roamed River's face.

"I'm not gonna start sobbing again," they said lightly. *Probably.*

Cassidy looked surprised. "I wasn't expecting you to."

Way to bring it up!

"Oh. Okay, well. Follow me."

The cat room was a large, open space with elaborate cat ramps and plastic tubes built along carpeted walls, through which the cats had access to the whole building. Charlie had built them all from scratch, and added to them whenever the whim struck him.

The addition of the television had been River's solution to the problem of all the cats trying to come sit with them upstairs on the bed when they watched. Now, they could curl up on cushions, watch from there, and everyone could keep an eye on them.

Cats leapt from all corners to greet River as they opened the door.

"Hello, babies!" they said, crouching down to greet everyone. Cassidy relieved them of the tray and set everything up while they were still dripping with cats.

"Okay, so, I thought we could hang out and watch something fun and eat cheese and play with cats," River said. "Does that sound okay?"

"Sounds heavenly," Cassidy said, then plopped himself on a cushion, long legs akimbo.

Mushroom leapt onto Cassidy's head, skinny white tail flicking his ear.

"Shit, sorry. Damn it, Mushroom, we've discussed this."

They plucked the cat off Cassidy's head and searched his scalp, moving his thick hair aside to search for any injury.

"You okay?"

"Mhm, feels good," Cassidy said, and shot River a flirtatious look.

Oh, damn. Be yourself, be yourself, beyourselfbeyourselfbeyourself.

"I'll be right back."

River fled the room, took some deep breaths, and grabbed the bag they'd prepared from behind the front desk. When they returned, Inspector Gadget, Murder Dog, and Grandma Fantastic had formed a loose arc around Cassidy waiting for his attention while Mushroom and Croissant crawled all over him. Typical. And fucking adorable.

"Aww."

"This is Inspector Gadget, right?" Cassidy asked, stroking her small head.

"That's her. Can you believe it? The vet, said she probably wouldn't have survived much longer than she did."

River sat on the cushion beside Cassidy and doled out chin scratches and ear scritches. There were some cats that demanded acknowledgement of their greatness upon entering a room.

Cassidy picked up Inspector Gadget and cradled her against his chest.

"Good job," he told the cat, and dropped a kiss on the missing tip of her ear.

River's heart melted.

Inspector Gadget stretched out her toes and flipped out of Cassidy's arms, only to scramble up his shoulder. He let her stay there and made himself another cracker.

"This guy dropped off all these old magazines along with his donation of towels and washcloths," River explained. "I like to cut them up while I watch something and make collages. Do you want to?"

Cassidy nodded enthusiastically.

"Very much. Idle hands being the devil's playthings and all that."

"ADHD hands, maybe?" River offered.

"Exactly."

They dug into the bag of magazines, glue, scissors, utility knives, and markers. Eventually, Inspector Gadget got annoyed at her perch moving and settled for curling up next to Cassidy's knee.

"No glitter?" Cassidy asked, pouting.

And somehow, Cassidy fucking Darling looked epically hot when he pouted. How was that fair? His plump lower lip glistened and his eyes went all soft and disappointed and River's brain short-circuited.

"If you just added a *k* you'd be Cassidy Darkling," they blurted.

Cassidy's pout was replaced with amusement.

"Darkling, I like that. If I could draw, I would want to write a comic book about Darkling."

"Ooh, what would Darkling's whole thing be?"

"Is it rude if I dig in?" Cassidy asked, indicating the cheese.

"Please do. And there's no glitter because cats."

"Oh, yes, bad combination."

"A lesson learned the hard way, unfortunately."

Cassidy grimaced, then drizzled honey over a cracker with brie and ate it in one bite. He groaned as he chewed and River felt it in their whole body—a shuddering promise of things to come. Hopefully.

"I think he'd be a splotch of ink that could flow around unnoticed on the ground, but then he could lift himself up and be any shape. So he could become the shape of a key or a rolling pin or a gun."

"In case it was a baking emergency?"

"Why would a gun help a baking emergency?" Cassidy retorted.

River grinned.

"I would definitely read that comic," they said, and turned on the TV. "I was thinking something light and fun? What do you like?"

Cassidy pointed at River's home screen.

"Wait, you watch *Secaucus Psychic*? I love that show."

"Really? Perfect."

River put on a random episode and familiar music filled the room. The cats settled down.

Cassidy held up a piece of blue cheese.

"If I eat this will you still want to kiss me?"

Heart pounding, River leaned closer. Close enough to see that Cassidy's rich brown irises had flecks of an even darker brown in them. Close enough to smell the shaving cream on his neck.

"What makes you think I wanna kiss you?" they murmured, eyes on Cassidy's mouth.

Then they leaned in slowly, brushed Cassidy's lips with their fingertips and watched his eyes flutter closed.

River kissed him gently, a slow, lingering kiss that said *more* and *yes* and sent warmth from River's mouth to their gut.

"Ask me now."

"If I eat this will you still want to kiss me?" he said, voice rough and low.

"Yeah."

Cassidy's expression raised the hair on River's arms. River settled onto their cushion and put together a cracker and cheese.

"You think I'd put something on my own cheese tray that would make me not wanna kiss you? Come on."

"So you *did* think about kissing me," Cassidy said.

River thought about laughing it off or denying it.

BE YOUR DAMN SELF.

"Yeah. I have thought about kissing you every day since our date."

"Shit, me too," Cassidy enthused. "Not in a creepy way."

"Me neither. No creeps here."

"Okay, what are you making," Cassidy asked, "and who's our dead person?"

"I think it's gonna be the blonde's brother," River theorized.

"Yeah, and at first she'll be like 'I miss him so much,' but then—"

"It'll turn out he, like, lost their whole inheritance in Atlantic City," River finished.

They both grinned at each other and River's cheeks heated.

River and Cassidy spent the next hour eating cheese, cutting things out of magazines from the late 1970s, and making increasingly absurd guesses about the happenings on *Secaucus Psychic*.

Cracker by cracker, joke by joke, and touch by touch, River relaxed.

CHAPTER 20

Cassidy

Cassidy was on the best date of his life. It had begun with death and crying, and now found him sprawled on the floor, fighting a cat called Mushroom for the last of the brie, but it was definitely the best.

Although he'd been the one to plan a dinner date, they weren't what he preferred. There was so much pressure on everything you said or did—the attempt to save yourself the pain of heartbreak by extrapolating who this person across from you was from a favorite book or their taste in salad dressing.

His ADHD went wild in such places, and he struggled to pick out his date's voice from among the hundreds of other sounds also present.

"Somehow," Cassidy said, razoring a capital B from its backdrop of orange dunes, "it never occurred to me that you were allowed to have a date where you just hang out and do crafts and play with cats."

"I know, right? I got the idea from my niece. She says grown-ups are stupid about fun and I think she might be right. I hate most of the stuff considered fun for adults, anyway."

"Yeah, I spend my time playing with animal skins and digging through bulk lots of glass eyes, so I'm with you there."

"Do you listen to music while you work on taxidermy projects?"

"I just started listening to audiobooks in the last few months when Nora showed me that you can change the speed. I had no idea. I'd get so distracted in the space between the words or sentences because I'd start thinking about other things. But now that I can listen to them double fast they finally going the speed of my brain. It's great."

"What are you reading right now?"

"A history of books that have been bound in human skin."

"Ooh, taxidermy adjacent."

"Yeah. I really like microhistories."

"And skin, apparently."

"You don't have to worry. You have beautiful skin, but the taxidermy of humans is illegal in all fifty states."

Cassidy grinned. River shot him an amused, flirtatious look that made him want to explore every inch of their skin (in a totally non-murdery way).

He peeked at what River was doing. While he had gone looking for color to use like strokes of paint, River had meticulously cut out objects and people and was playing with their arrangement by moving them around.

"What are you making?"

"Oh, uh. Every year my friend makes a vision board. I know, it's so cheesy, but she says it helps when she forces herself to get specific about her desires. It's easy to not acknowledge a goal or desire because we're scared we can't have it. So the act of making a vision board is about getting specific about what you want and what your dreams are. Then you hang it somewhere you'll see it a lot so you're always reminded of them."

River ran their fingertips over the images they'd cut out. Onscreen, a new episode of *Secaucus Psychic* began.

"Banger of a theme," River said, suddenly self-conscious.

"I love this idea," Cassidy said, shoving his palette of magazine colors to the side and grabbing the next magazine off the stack, mind already flooded with goals, dreams, questions.

They watched the episode companionably, each working on their own vision board. As Jackie, the medium, communed with the spirit of a dog-walker who loved gambling and Billy Joel, they passed scissors, glue sticks, and markers back and forth. By unspoken agreement, they kept their eyes on their own papers.

Mostly.

As that episode turned into another, Cassidy started peeking over at River's vision board.

"Will you tell me about this?"

River nodded, hair falling in waves that hid their face. Cassidy leaned in and ever so slowly tucked River's hair behind their ear. They shivered and pressed closer. The space between them felt warmer than the ambient air in that way that promised chemistry.

"Mine's general, not just about this coming year."

They pointed to an image of a huge red barn in the middle of rolling hills, a jagged tree line in the background. They'd glued pictures of chicken coops, raised garden beds, and flowers surrounding it.

"I really want my own place someday," they said, voice tender and eyes dreamy. "I want to be able to have as many animals as I want, and pick flowers in my yard. I read a book once where this lady would buy fresh flowers for her whole house every week and I've always wanted to have them. I want to be able to adopt a hundred cats if I feel like it."

Cassidy could picture River, feet bare, hair blowing wild in the breeze, hands in the dirt, sowing the seeds of the flowers they would cut for their own pleasure later as cats they'd saved sunned themself around the garden.

They touched pictures of beautiful people in an array of styles.

"I want to feel comfortable in my own skin. I don't know exactly what that would look like. Or feel like. But I ..."

Want it, need it, crave it. That was what River's face communicated.

"I want the space to figure it out," they concluded with a nod.

The rest of the vision board was a swirl of color—flowers, plants, art, colors, animals.

"I know I'm supposed to, but I don't have any big dream of a career. I don't want to be famous. I don't want to order people around. I just want to live and make my own decisions and be happy. God, that sounds so cheesy," they groaned.

"No way! I'm smiling over here, you just can't see because your hair is like the blinkers they put on horses."

River snorted and glanced up through their hair, smiling at Cassidy's smile.

"I fully endorse a life made of just living," he said. "So it's only out of curiosity that I ask: when you were a kind was there something you wanted to be when you grew up?"

River's smile was wry.

"I wanted to do the weather."

"On TV?"

"God, no. I thought the weather people got to go outside and stand in different parts of the region and report what the weather was. As in, 'I'm in Garnet Run and it's about twenty degrees here. The wind is coming in from the west at whatever miles an hour.' When I found out they just read the info off a screen?" They shook their head in mock tragedy. "Dream crushed."

"I'm so sorry for your loss."

"That's what I'm saying, though. I was born without the ambition gene. Even people who work totally normal jobs *also* have a TikTok with 10,000 followers who watch their passion of, like, re-caning chairs with plastic cord made from non-recyclable plastic, spun by hand on a loom they built themselves in the tradition of their Norwegian great-grandmother."

Cassidy laughed.

"You don't much strike me as the exhibitionist type."

"I'm not. I run the shelter Instagram and I don't even like it if my reflection is visible in a cat's water bowl in a picture." They shuddered. "People think if you don't have career ambition then you must have some passion project that you're just waiting to throw your time into. And if you don't have that, then you're a loser. I shouldn't care what people think, I know," River said presumptively.

"I wasn't gonna say that," Cassidy protested. "I was going to say that lots of folks don't really feel like they exist or matter without seeing themselves through others' eyes. But if what you want are time and space to figure out how to feel comfortable in your own skin, to take care of animals and the land, and to relish your short time on earth, sounds like the last thing you'd want is to feel self-consciousness in front of people watching."

"Yeah," River said. "Exactly. And being nonbinary in a small town in Wyoming doesn't exactly lend itself to the desire to be watched."

"Can I ask a question about that?" When River nodded, Cassidy asked, "What does it feel like?"

"To be nonbinary?"

"Mhm. Is that okay to ask?"

"Yeah, it's fine to ask, just hard to answer, cuz it's different for everyone. Um, well, okay, what does being a man feel like to you?"

Cassidy tried on and discarded multiple characteristics, but they were all external—markers of masculinity, detritus of the patriarchal culture they lived in. There was nothing that felt essential. No quality, belief, desire, or thought he could point to and say *That. That right there is the seat of my maleness.*

"I don't know, actually," he said after a while, grimacing. "I just kinda ... feel it?"

"Yeah, so that feeling, that knowing deep down, I don't have it. I've never had it. Growing up perceived as a boy, I didn't feel maleness. Some trans friends of mine had kind of the opposite feeling, where they just *felt* their gender deep inside them—just as intrinsically as you feel maleness—only it didn't match their birth sex. But I didn't really feel that way either. I feel like I float around in a pool of gender and sometimes I'll float through one and sometimes through another but they're never quite distinct or consistent. That's kind of the best I can explain it."

Cassidy felt gears in his head click into place, effigies to a certain order that he had inherited falling away like sand.

"Thanks. It's interesting that I can know strongly that I'm male but not be able to know why at all, and you can know strongly that you *aren't*. So for both of us there is something that we can recognize as this thing, but it's not tangible, we just ... I'm not sure what I'm trying to say."

Something that felt so crystalline in his head splintered when he tried to put it into words.

"I think I know what you mean," River said. "It's kind of similar to faith, maybe? Not religious faith necessarily, but a conviction. We can agree on a general enough notion of how faith functions so that we can talk about it, but it can't ever be pinned down by definition. So it's always gonna be a thing that we reference through a combination of metaphor and assumption."

"It does feel kind of like faith," Cassidy said. "I can't show any proof to back up feeling, but I know it's true anyway."

River nodded, gaze moving from his eyes to his lips. Heat pooled in Cassidy's groin.

"So what about yours?"

"My ..." Cassidy played the last few moments back in his head. Had he missed something? "Gender?" he tried.

"Your vision board," River said, smiling.

"Oh, right." Cassidy dragged his mind back to his hopes and dreams. "I don't remember if I told you at Craftmas, but I used to work as a carpenter."

"Oh, right, Charlie said."

"Yeah. I started in high school and did it until about a year ago. I'd done taxidermy as a hobby for years, but more and more people were bringing me animals they wanted me to mount, or asking for commissions. A few years ago, Nora started shifting her own art interests and they began to overlap with mine more and more."

"What kind of stuff did she used to do?"

"Large metalwork pieces that took her months to finish. They were absolutely stunning—I have one in my house that I can show you next time we're there."

The assumption tripped off his tongue before he realized he'd made it, but River's eyes lit and Cassidy knew there would be a next time.

"We began vending together because it was cheaper to share a table, but as our work converged, we found new ways draw in a more diverse pool of customers, which helped both of us sell more. Exponentially. Enough so that about a year ago I quit my job to do it full time."

"Damn, that's amazing."

Every time Cassidy told the story he was flooded with gratitude for his current position.

"Yeah, it's been a dream come true. I liked carpentry fine, but I didn't have passion for it. Nora hates being told what to do *ever*, so she's been fired from or quit just about any job you could think of."

"Awesome," River said.

"Suffice it to say that self-employment suits us both. Wait, what was your question? Oh, the vision board, right."

He tapped a picture of a quaint, old-fashioned general store.

"When the events are inside, the fluorescents kill me. Doing the summer art and craft fair circuits is better because they're outside. But you need to sell a lot of product to make a profit after the expense of traveling to get to them. And speaking of traveling, it's a *lot*. And I'm more of a stay-at-home guy."

"Very relatable," River said.

"Eventually, I would love to be able to stop doing as many fairs and get a permanent storefront. A place where I could have the work out for sale in addition to shipping orders and vending. Just something simple, like this."

He traced the lines of the general store's weathered wood. It reminded him of a certain patina that bones got while in the process of being bleached by the sun.

"Wow, yes," River said. "You totally should. Your stuff is amazing. So's Nora's. I don't wanna bust into your vision board, but have you thought about selling prints of your work?"

"Like posters?"

"Like art prints. You would get someone to photograph your pieces, edit the images until you're happy with them, and then you have another income stream. You could have some that are framed already hung around the shop, and you could have all the prints available loose and for cheaper."

Yes! Different sizes, mugs and notepads and greeting cards, and images of the work to put on the website.

His brain clicked away with dozens of ideas, so many ideas he worried he'd lose them.

River passed him a piece of construction paper and a marker and he jotted down the storm.

"You," Cassidy said, "are a freaking genius."

CHAPTER 21

River

Giddy with excitement for Cassidy and delight at how well the date was going, River flopped onto their back with a satisfied sigh.

Instantly, they were mobbed by cats. Cactus Face was purring like a motorboat, making biscuits on River's hair. Winston draped his body over their shins for some reason. It didn't seem at all comfortable to River. Reishi and Enoki pounced on their stomach, and Murder Dog was attempting to burrow into their spleen.

"Please don't murder River in the middle of our date," Cassidy requested of the cats. Then, to River, "Do you need assistance?"

His face appeared above them, amusement apparent.

"Nah, I'm good. They're just little flop bears, aren't you?"

Cactus Face yawned against River's skull and Winston flopped even more. River held out a hand and Cassidy tugged them upright. He didn't let go immediately, but squeezed River's hand. They squeezed back.

"Do you want some of this?" River asked, bringing out the weed and pipe. "It's an indica-dominant hybrid."

"I don't know what that means, but yes please."

They passed the pipe back and forth.

"You know what would be so good right now," Cassidy mused. "One of those huge popcorn tubs."

"Omigod!"

River darted out of the room and toward the kitchen slash cat supply area. But as they passed the front desk and the windows that looked out on the parking lot and the woods beyond, they saw a world inverted. The parking lot, usually black, was white. Snow was already deep on the ground and falling so heavily that night almost looked like day.

The fucking blizzard. In all the emotional chaos of the evening, they'd forgotten about Charlie's warning.

They grabbed the popcorn from the kitchen and did a cursory supply check. They should be okay for a few days at least.

"The good news," River said when they reentered the cat room. They held up the popcorn.

"Oh, damn, you popcorn angel. I just realized you never told me about dropping off the others—how did people react? Wait, is there bad news?"

"Depends on your attitude and your plans, I suppose," River stalled. "There's a blizzard. Which I forgot about. And I have no clue what time it is or how long we've been in here, but there's already about a foot. How's your truck in the snow?"

Cassidy's eyes had widened at *blizzard* and he stood to go look for himself.

"Oh. Yup."

River held out the tub of popcorn and Cassidy bent and breathed in the smell. He took a handful of caramel corn and a handful of buttered popcorn and ate the two together.

"As good as you remember it?"

Cassidy moaned in the affirmative and desire tightened in River's stomach.

They sat down on either side of the tub and ate handfuls of popcorn as they watched the snow fall.

"Maybe you should stay here," River offered. "Weed and snow and driving in the dark. Bad idea."

"Definitely," Cassidy agreed. "I'd need to wait an hour or so and by then the snow will probably be too deep."

"Okay, so it's decided, then. You'll stay."

Cassidy smiled slowly and River had the distinct sensation of having crossed a threshold, passed over into an after, thereby describing a before.

Or maybe they were just really stoned.

"I'll stay."

"What are you doing for Christmas this year?" Cassidy asked.

Outside, the snow fell and fell. Inside, it was warm and cozy. They were lying on the floor of the cat room again, passing the pipe while the cats used them as furniture.

River snorted.

"That excited, huh?"

"I don't see my parents anymore," River said. "But now that my brother moved back I'll probably spend it with him, Wes, and Gus. That's what I did last year. It's relaxing and non-horrible, unlike Christmas with my parents used to be."

"What kind of horrible are your parents?" Cassidy asked.

River sighed.

"I know how lucky I am. So many people have it way worse."

"Meh, those people aren't here and I care about you."

River allowed themself a moment to bask in that.

"My dad is mean. And kind of scary. It's not what he does—although it's also what he does—but this whole energy he gives off. It's ..."

They shivered.

"It's hard to explain, but there's something about him that always makes me feel like whatever I say or do might be ignored or it might make him say horrible, nasty, insulting things. Just the way he looks at me—looked at me—the scorn was palpable."

"Because of gender stuff, or how you dress, or?"

"Oh, I have never mentioned anything about gender to my parents."

River couldn't even imagine what they'd have been on the receiving end of if their dad had ever known.

"A few years ago when I met Rye, I was living at home. Well, mostly. It was totally miserable so sometimes I'd sleep in my friend Tracy's car. There was no way I could afford college and all I did was get high and kick rocks around empty parking lots with my friends. It was grim."

Nights so long and lonely they stayed up and watched the sun rise to convince themself there was still beauty and sense in the world. Scouring the internet for information about how they were feeling and what it meant. Finding support online that probably saved their life, but knowing those people were hundreds or thousands of miles away—too far for a hug, a hand squeeze, a midnight rescue.

"The way he looked at me, though. Like, he didn't know what he knew, but I could tell he thought something was off. He knew Adam was gay and had no problem telling him what he thought about that. I guess he probably thought I was too. And whenever he'd look at me I could see this query in his eye, like he was trying to figure out what the precise thing was that made me a freak. I started dressing in baggy stuff to look kind of skater-y so that I could grow my hair out and he'd think it was a style choice."

"I don't see you much as a skater."

"Oh, definitely not," River laughed. "I'd die."

"What about your mom?"

"If she weren't married to my dad maybe she'd be an okay person?"

River couldn't imagine her outside the equation of the family she'd created.

"But she just went along with whatever he said, even when I could tell she didn't agree. Even after my sister had Gus—"

"Your sister is Gus' mom?"

"Yeah, Marina. I think she knew that she wasn't going to be able to be a parent, but she hoped so hard that maybe having a baby would force her to be? Anyway, she wasn't able to get clean and Adam adopted Gus when she was a baby. Which is awesome for everyone. But anyway, my mom wanted to raise the baby as their own after Marina left but my dad wouldn't agree. Said it was Marina's mess and she'd clean it up or pay the consequences."

Cassidy shook his head. "Yeah, it definitely wouldn't be the baby who paid the consequences."

"Funny how he didn't seem to care about the baby at all, huh? Pretty in character. And my mom capitulated. They didn't even know I'd called Adam until he showed up at the house with Marina's permission to take the baby. He was living in Boulder then, so he took Gus back there."

"But your mom was excited? To be a grandparent?"

"My mom's never precisely excited about anything. She's kind of a mystery to me. It's like she doesn't care about anything so that she's not disappointed, no matter what happens?"

"Sounds like a useful defense mechanism if she was prepared to have to go along with anything your dad decreed."

River nodded. They'd discussed this with Adam often enough.

"Adam thinks our dad picked her because she's so malleable. They never fight because she never stands her ground about anything."

"That sounds pretty dismal."

"Right!? She's like a zombie. I have a sick fascination with what's going on inside her head. Like, I've fantasized about getting her really stoned and seeing if she'd let her guard drop. But, ya know, then I'd have to spend time with her."

"What's she like when you're alone?"

"It's been years. But when I was younger she'd just kind of chatter about nothing. Whatever she was doing or who she'd seen at the supermarket or what was on sale. It was all mind-numbingly dull, and I couldn't tell if she wanted me to answer her or if she was just talking to herself, which meant I was always on edge."

River remembered trying to engage her by responding and seeing the surprise in her face as she remembered they were listening.

"And she would never answer any of what she called personal questions, which could be anything from 'How old were you when you and Dad got married?' to 'Do you prefer cats or dogs?', and she refused to entertain hypotheticals. If I asked something like 'Where would you want to live if you didn't live in Wyoming?' she would be like, 'But I do live in Wyoming.' So, I don't actually know that much about her. It's kinda sad. Not that she knows me either."

Once, this had made River feel exceptionally lonely. Living in a house with two people you were forcibly connected to but shared nothing with made River feel like a fist, clenched so tight they ached.

Cassidy rolled onto his side toward River.

"Her incredible loss," he said, and kissed River's cheek.

River rolled toward him so they were facing one another and buried their face in Cassidy's neck. Cassidy's arms came around them and it felt so natural, so right to be held by him.

"So yeah, no family Christmas for me. What about you?"

Cassidy shifted them so that River was lying in the crook of his arm. They moved slowly to avoid squishing the cats.

"My mom died two years ago."

River squeezed him.

"I'm so sorry. Unless you felt about her the way I feel about my mom. In that case, I don't mean to presume."

They could feel the vibrations of Cassidy's soft chuckle through his chest.

"She was complicated, but mostly great," he said. "Neither she or my dad ever cared much about Christmas, so it was never a big thing when I was a kid. The last couple years it's been easy to let it go. My dad's ... He's a very kind man, very generous. But he's not really present. Any time you talk to him it's like you're pulling him out of his real life, which is in his head."

"Is that since your mom died, or always?"

"Always, but it's become more consistent as he's gotten older. We hired a nurse who looks in on him a few times a week, but pretty soon we're gonna have to discuss something more full-time."

For a moment, Cassidy looked like a lost little boy. Then he sat up and waggled his fingers to the nearest cats. Inspector Gadget took him up on this gambit and began dive-bombing his hand.

"My dad hates the idea of an assisted living facility," he said. "We'd have to drag him there kicking and screaming. I don't know, maybe we'll be able to afford a full-time live-in aide."

River raised their eyebrows and said gently, "I think those are pretty expensive. I'm so glad you and Nora are doing well with the business but ..."

They trailed off, not wanting to deflate Cassidy, but he just nodded.

"Yeah, we have money set aside for it. It's ..." He ran a hand through his hair. "A little weird."

"Weird, like you accidentally made a ton of money on crypto? Weird, like you robbed a bank, or?"

Cassidy nodded. "Yeah, I robbed a bank. You won't turn me in will you?"

"Your crimes are safe with me," they said.

"It's actually weird like my mom wrote this song years ago. Kind of a one-hit wonder. About five years ago, a show contacted her about using the song in an episode. She said yes, but the show got stalled in production and didn't end up coming out until after she died. Then the show turned out to be really big and after the episode with her song in it aired, tons of people started streaming it and it was on the soundtrack."

A smile played at the corners of Cassidy's mouth.

"It was kind of cool for me, actually," he said. "Because there was a Riven song on the soundtrack and I've always been a big fan."

"Wait, seriously?" River was delighted. "That's amazing. I can't wait to tell Rye. He loves Riven; he'll totally flip at that. What show was it?"

"*Velvet.*"

"Holy shit. That's major."

"Yeah, so Nora and I control the publishing and licensing rights for her work, so we're using the revenue to pay for the nurse and for whatever else my dad will need going forward. The money's not endless, but it's been really damn helpful."

"Put it on!"

"The song?"

"Yeah, of course the song. I wanna hear your mom's hit."

Cassidy's smile was warm and he pulled out his phone.

While Croissant and Mushroom made biscuits on their thigh, River listened to a song that was folky and synth-y and very catchy.

Cassidy's expression was one of pride and when he caught River looking, his eyes heated.

"Hey," he said softly, scooting a bit closer.

River put a hand between his shoulder blades and ran their palm gently down his spine. They could feel the shiver run through him.

Cassidy—big, strong, sweet Cassidy—looked undone by a single touch.

"I don't want to be weird and make a move on you while we're listening to your mom," River said. "But I'm just saying that I *do* wanna make a move on you."

River laughed at the speed with which Cassidy cut the music and tossed his phone across the floor, where it was immediately taken for a cat toy.

"Yes, please. I want a move to be made on me."

River smiled and led him upstairs.

CHAPTER 22

Cassidy

Cassidy followed River up the narrow staircase to their room, enjoying the view of their gorgeous round ass in his face.

Their room was dark and small, with a bed, a dresser with a TV on top, a small bookcase, a closet, and a bathroom. River flipped a switch and the space flickered with the soft glow of fairy lights nestled along the ceiling. The whimsical lighting transformed the whole room.

"Oh, wow."

"I was the lucky recipient of Gus' reject lights last year," River said. "They weren't bright or colorful enough for her purposes but they were perfect for mine."

They stepped into the bathroom and began brushing their teeth.

"No fair," Cassidy protested. "Now you'll be minty fresh and I'll have blue cheese breath."

"I think I have ..." River rummaged around under the sink. "Here."

They handed him the twin to their own toothbrush. It was purple and sparkly and had a little grip for your thumb, and it filled Cassidy with absurd tenderness to imagine River picking them out.

He thanked them and brushed his teeth. When he set the toothbrush down on the edge of the sink, he couldn't help but imagine it sitting there in the future—his own toothbrush for when he spent the night at River's.

River's arms snaked around his waist. They hugged him from behind, pressing their weight against him, and laid a cheek on his back.

"Cassidy," they said softly, and it was a complete sentence.

He turned in their embrace.

River's eyes were a bottomless blue sea, their lips plump berries. Their hair fell around their face, messy and perfect.

"Damn."

He kissed those berry lips softly at first, then River's tongue caressed his, and the kiss turned heated.

River stepped back against the wall and Cassidy caged them there as they kissed again, nearly lightheaded from the lust that tore through him.

He kissed River's throat and their breath caught.

"You like your neck kissed?"

River nodded, baring their neck.

Cassidy obliged, drinking in their shiver.

"What else do you like?" he asked, nuzzling them and placing a kiss on the soft skin below their ear. "Or not like. I want to make you feel good."

River groaned and led him to the bed, pushing him down and straddling his hips. Jesus, that was hot. He dragged his mind back to the information he wanted.

"Tell me," he murmured.

"I like, um, stuff up my ass. I really like getting oral, but ... I don't like to use, like, penis-y words."

Cassidy nodded and stroked their back.

"Thanks. Are there words you'd like me to use."

"I'd like you to refer to my genitalia as the Titan of Industry."

Cassidy blinked. Of course he would use whatever language River found affirming, but he had to admit he hadn't been expecting that.

"All right, thanks."

"Oh my god, I'm messing with you," River said, laughing. "Sorry, just a little nonbinary humor to break the tension."

Cassidy laughed.

"Tension broken," he said.

"Anyway, I'm still figuring that out," they said.

"Okay." Cassidy stroked their cheek. "Keep me informed."

River nodded. "What about you? What do you like?"

Visions of all the things he wanted to do with River flooded Cassidy's mind.

"Fuck," he breathed.

"Could you be more specific?"

"Ha ha. Well, since you mentioned putting things up your ass and oral, there's kind of this picture in my mind that I'd like to explore."

River's pupils blew and they swayed, lips parting. Cassidy steadied them with a hand on either hip.

"Do you have toys you like to use?"

River nodded and opened the drawer of the bedside table. The brought out a red toy flecked with glitter.

"You like glitter everywhere but in your crafts, huh?"

"What? Oh. Yeah, there's just something about fucking yourself with glitter. This one vibrates. You could control it inside me, if you want."

Cassidy's cock jumped and he groaned. River often struck Cassidy as a bit shy, so to hear them talk frankly about getting fucked with a glittery vibrator was getting to him.

"Yeah, I think we could probably make that happen." He cleared his throat and attempted to control his breathing.

They kissed hotly, tongues caressing, fingers tangling in hair, limbs entwining. Cassidy felt like he was going to explode without even being touched, he was so turned on by River's body against his. River was an enthusiastic lover and they touched Cassidy with an expression of intent concentration that was endearing and gratifying. It was like they drank in each response Cassidy gave and applied it to their touch, turning him on even more.

"Let me touch you?" he asked, needing to cool off.

River nodded and Cassidy slid a hand up their back, feeling smooth skin and the wings of their shoulder blades.

"Want this off?" Cassidy tugged on the hem of their shirt.

River stripped it off and Cassidy laved their nipples hungrily. River shook in their arms and groaned when he sucked a mark up next to their nipple.

"This okay, baby?"

River groaned in affirmation and pulled Cassidy's shirt off too. When their chests came together they both gasped. River's head fell back and their breath came faster.

"Lube?" Cassidy asked, already fumbling in the drawer the vibrator had come from.

River nodded and knelt up, stripping off the rest of their clothes.

"Fuck," they said. "I want you so much."

"Me too, baby. Jesus. You're so gorgeous."

River's lashes swept down and they smiled a private smile.

"You are too."

They handed Cassidy the vibrator.

"This is big," he said.

River blinked, squirming.

Cassidy's arousal ratcheted up a notch, his voice going dark.

"You like to be filled up?"

River nodded and when they spoke their voice was rough.

"I don't want to be able to get away from it."

"From the vibrator?"

"The pleasure."

Fuck, fuck, fuck.

Cassidy groaned. "Well, that's extremely fucking hot. Please allow me to oblige."

River rolled off them and lay on the mattress, legs spread. Cassidy wanted to consume them.

"Tell me if I do anything you don't like, okay?"

River nodded and Cassidy spread lube on his fingers. He traced River's hole and they shuddered and closed their eyes. Spots of flush reddened their cheeks. *Get on with it*, their whole body was screaming.

Cassidy opened River up slowly, relishing the gasps and groans as he went.

"'M ready," River breathed, pulling their legs apart.

"Jesus Christ. Okay."

Cassidy slid the vibrator slowly inside River. They panted as it penetrated them deeper and deeper. Cassidy angled the toy experimentally and River cried out.

He watched their body stretch around the thick toy and didn't think he'd ever been harder in his life.

"Oh, fuck," River moaned. "Oh, fuck, fuck yes."

"This what you like," Cassidy said. "Being fucked open until there's nothing you can do to escape the pleasure?"

River whimpered. "Yes."

Cassidy slid the vibrator out and back in again, this time angling it to watch the exact moment River felt everything. They had their head thrown back and were panting, and Cassidy didn't think he'd ever seen anyone as beautiful.

Cassidy pressed the vibrator deep inside and pressed the button on the base. River convulsed and grabbed for Cassidy's shoulder.

"Oh my god." Their eyes were wide and shocked.

Every time he pulled the toy out River writhed, seeking the sensation, and every time he pressed it deep, River groaned, hips flexing.

"Can I taste you?" Cassidy asked, touching River's hip softly.

They nodded enthusiastically, so Cassidy held the vibrator in with one hand and held himself up with the other. Then he lowered himself to taste River's flesh. When his tongue made contact, River punched their hips up. They tasted of salt and sugar, and Cassidy explored every inch.

"Oh, god," River groaned. "Oh, fuck."

Cassidy hummed his gratification and River shuddered. River writhed between the vibrator and Cassidy's clever mouth.

When Cassidy moved up to kiss River, his cock rested on the vibrator and stars exploded in his gut. The sensation was exquisite.

River cupped him and rubbed until Cassidy gasped.

"Will you fuck me with this," they asked, giving his cock a gentle squeeze.

Cassidy groaned. "You sure?"

River closed their eyes happily and nodded, humming as they removed the vibrator.

Clothes off, Cassidy reached into the drawer again. He'd felt condoms in there when he'd grabbed the lube.

"Vibrator's about the same size as you," River mused as they watched him put on the condom.

Cassidy found himself at a loss for words. He kissed River instead.

"How would you like it?" he asked.

By way of reply, River sat up and guided Cassidy's cock to their ass. Then they lowered themself slowly onto his erection. Their mouth was slack and open and their eyes rolled back in their head as they came to rest on Cassidy's hips with his cock buried inside them.

The sensation of River's velvet hot body clutching him as he moved was liquid and heavenly. They both shuddered.

"You are so beautiful," Cassidy murmured, brushing his thumb over River's plump lips.

"You make me feel beautiful," River said, then squeezed their eyes shut and began to move.

Cassidy angled his hips and River moaned and shivered.

Cassidy felt like if he never accomplished anything else in his life, if he could make River Mills feel good, he could die happy.

"River, fuck," Cassidy moaned, their body hugging his cock exquisitely. "You wanna touch yourself?"

"Change places," River said, breathless.

Cassidy held River tightly and flipped them so he was on top. They both groaned as this new position brought them into new, electrifying contact. Cassidy slid up to kiss River. They opened to him, sucking desperately on his tongue.

River finally broke the kiss and, with an impish expression, reached into the drawer and drew out another vibrator. They raised their eyebrows in question and Cassidy nodded, too turned on to form words.

The toy buzzed to life. Holding Cassidy's gaze, River dragged it slowly down their body, eyelashes fluttering when it reached between their legs.

"Holy shit, Cassidy."

River moved the vibrator down and Cassidy started. As River used the toy on themselves, they were using it on Cassidy too. It was placed so that he felt its buzz in the root of his cock when he was inside River. When he pulled out, it dragged against the sensitive skin of his cock, driving him back into River's heat.

River put a hand on Cassidy's back to stop his thrusts while he was deep inside them. Then they pressed the vibrator tighter between them where it pressed into Cassidy's pubic bone.

"Oh my fucking god," Cassidy exclaimed. He rocked, staying deep inside River but not losing contact with the glorious vibration.

"Cassidy," River said. They looked scared. "I'm gonna come."

Cassidy redoubled his efforts.

"I'm gonna ... oh god, oh god, ohgod."

Cassidy felt River's orgasm hit. Their ass clamped around his cock and every muscle in their body seemed to tighten. At the height of their orgasm, River reached for Cassidy's hand, squeezing it tight.

"Oh, fuck, Cassidy, please don't stop, please keep fucking me."

Cassidy was wild with lust and affection and the desire to give River pleasure. He thrust deep inside River as they came and came, milking his cock.

"Oh my god," River groaned.

Cassidy groaned too.

"I'm really close," he ground out.

River didn't answer, just clenched their ass around his erection and groaned again, shivering.

Cassidy brought his awareness back to his own body as the pleasure grew more and more intense, until it peaked in an orgasm so strong it was almost painful.

He was panting, sweat trickling down his back, and his legs felt like jelly. But the orgasm rolled through him like a wave and he didn't surface until it had passed.

"Jesus fucking Christ," he breathed, collapsing next to River.

"Wow," River said.

Cassidy buried his face in River's neck and breathed in the scent of their skin and sweat until his breathing slowed. River pulled the covers up.

"Comfy?" they murmured.

"So comfy. You okay?"

He felt River nod.

"You?"

"I'm stupendous," Cassidy admitted. "You want me to get the lights?"

River reached around the corner of the bed and then they were in darkness. Cassidy searched for their mouth and ended up planting a kiss on their nostrils.

"Oops."

"Cassidy?"

"Yeah, baby."

"Thanks. For ... that was ... I appreciate ... You did what I asked and ..."

They kissed his cheek.

"Of course," Cassidy said.

He didn't even want to contemplate that anyone had *not* treated River the way they asked to be treated because then he'd end up in jail.

"Good night," River whispered.

"Good night, River. This was the best date of my life."

River nestled closer and Cassidy was almost asleep when they heard a soft, "Mine too."

Cassidy was wrenched from a dream into a nightmare. At least, that's what it felt like was happening, since he'd been awakened by some kind of horrible monster with claws and fangs and glowing eyes.

"God damn it, not my fucking neck!"

"What? How? Who?" Cassidy blurted, flailing to try and find the offending beast and slay it before it could harm River further.

He connected with something and heard an "Oof."

"Shit, River?"

The fairy lights came on and illuminated a scene rather different from the gnashing bloodbath Cassidy had expected. A single medium-sized cat was sprawled on River. It was purring louder than Cassidy had known it was possible for a cat to purr, and trying to make biscuits on River's throat.

"Soooo," River said. "I forgot to tell you something."

They sat up and scooped the cat—was it Cactus Face?—into their arms like a baby. The purring intensified.

River turned to Cassidy with the most adorable *Eep* face and Cassidy melted. River could say that they had a kink where they loved being scratched by cats in the middle of the night and Cassidy would nod and be like, *Sounds great, babe* and go back to sleep.

"There's this tunnel—would you call it a tunnel? Maybe it's more of a tube. Anyway."

They pointed to the wall where Cassidy realized that what he'd thought was a framed painting of a black circle on a field of white was *actually* a picture frame hung around a circular opening in the wall itself.

"It goes from downstairs and lets the cats come visit me. And Cactus Face does this cute thing where sometimes she'll come sleep on my chest and cuddle. But recently she's started making biscuits on my neck and I guess she was startled when she got on the bed and you were there and she probably just freaked out. Sorry."

If Cactus Face—yay, he'd been right—had been surprised to find him there, did that mean River didn't bring many people back here? Or brought them back but didn't invite them to stay the night?

That was not the point so Cassidy dragged his mind back to reality.

"That sounds uncomfortable," he said.

"It's not my favorite place to be stomped on," they said. Then, "Litotes! I knew I'd remember."

"Uh."

"The term for when you understate something by saying the opposite. I was trying to remember it at Craftmas. Anyway, yeah. I don't know why she does it. Sorry she freaked you out."

"It's okay, I wasn't that freaked out."

River raised an eyebrow. In their arms, Cactus Face also seemed to raise an eyebrow, then jumped down onto the bed.

"I thought you were being torn apart by Cenobites or consumed by fire ants or something," River said, grinning.

"Ahh."

River's kiss was an instant balm. He slid his fingers into their soft hair and massaged their scalp.

"Mmm," River murmured and they both lay down.

Cactus Face yawned, turned in a circle twice, then plopped down between River and Cassidy.

"Aww," Cassidy said. "She wants to be between us."

It was extremely adorable and also Cassidy dearly wanted to

yeet her out of bed so that he could pull River close, stroke their hair and their back and kiss their lips. But before he could do anything but drop a hand on Cactus Face's soft fluff, he sank into blissful sleep.

CHAPTER 23

River

Rye and Charlie's holiday party the next week started off with a bang when Rye explained to everyone that he'd seen a tutorial about how to cut open champagne with a sword and that he was going to try it.

"Do you *have* a sword?" Jack asked, sounding impressed.

"No," Charlie answered for him. Then he turned to his boyfriend. "Wait, do you?"

"No, but I've got a knife and a knife is basically a sword, only shorter."

"I don't think that's necessarily true," Zachary protested, but Rye had already run to get the champagne. He turned to the rest of the group and explained, "There's a practice called sabering that's done with a knife, though. It's often performed for the awe of people who are dazzled by things like opening bottles, I believe."

Wes laughed at that and Bram seemed genuinely interested, gazing at his boyfriend tenderly.

"Okay, who wants to hold the bottle for me?" Rye asked, returning with a bottle held aloft. His eyes were bright with excitement as he scanned the room.

River exchanged dubious glances with everyone. They adored

Rye and believed he could do almost anything he put his mind to. But he wasn't what they'd call coordinated.

When no one volunteered, Cassidy cleared his throat.

"I guess I will?"

Wait, what?

River clutched his arm, attempting to telegraph that this would be a grave error.

"Er, should we have safety goggles or other protective face coverings?" Cassidy asked.

"No," Charlie said. "Because you're not doing it. "

Relief coursed through River—and through Cassidy if the relaxation of all his muscles was any indication.

"Babe," Charlie said to Rye gently. "You're not swinging a kitchen knife at a glass bottle six inches from someone's hand. Yesterday you fell out of the shower."

"How, though?" Simon asked softly. Jack snickered.

Rye sniffed. "I'm not sure why you'd bring that up. Fine, I'll hold it myself."

Charlie held his hands up in resignation and stepped away. Rye wasn't unreasonable, but once he got an idea in his head it would be seen to fruition.

Cassidy reached for River's hand and squeezed it. Between them, though new, was the sense that neither were experiencing this moment alone; they were connected. River had always wondered what it would feel like to have that, and now that they did, they could drop a line to their past self that it felt fucking fantastic.

Rye played around with the grip on the bottle and the knife for a moment and while he was looking down, the group collectively took several steps away from him.

"Oh, this is actually easier anyway. Okay!"

Rye waggled his eyebrows at the group. Then he guided the knife along the bottle to hit the neck and, like magic, the top of the bottle fell to the floor, cork inside it.

There was a collective gasp.

"Holy shit, you cut open the champagne with a knife," Jack said unnecessarily.

Rye accepted their accolades and their apologies for doubting him gracefully, then turned to River and made the cross-eyed, tongue lolling face that River thought of as his *Good thing that went my way cuz I was majorly bluffing* face. River gave him a thumbs up turned away, grimacing.

Their group was close, but River hadn't worried about bringing Cassidy into the fold because he got along so well with people. (They hadn't realized what they'd need to worry about would actually be a knife-wielding Rye.) Cassidy was at ease with everyone and made them feel at ease in return. It was one of the things River liked about him so much.

"What's got you blushing?" Simon asked, taking up his usual party post of leaning against the wall with River.

River's hands flew to their cheeks.

"Shut up."

They stood in companionable silence, gazing at their friends.

"What do you think?" River asked quietly.

Simon didn't talk much in group settings, which meant he always noticed more than everyone else.

"He reminds me of an eager kid, really open and unselfconscious. But it's tempered by confidence."

"Maybe too much confidence if he's volunteering to get his hand chopped off," River grumbled, but they were mostly kidding.

"He wanted us to like him," Simon said.

"Er, did it work?" River asked.

"I'd say so."

"There are a truly delicious number of queers in this town," Rye said, slinging his arm over River's shoulder.

Rye had taken a chance on River when they needed it the most, given them a job and a place to live, and trusted them. They spent a lot of time together at the shelter. If he didn't like Cassidy, it would really suck.

"So what do you think?" River asked, at the same time as Rye said, "I like your boyfriend."

"Oh, thank god," River said.

"Thank god, what?" asked Jack, with a kiss to Simon's cheek.

"That I like Cassidy," Rye said.

Jack nodded dispassionately. "He hasn't annoyed me yet."

"Everything annoys you," Charlie said, coming up behind his brother. "Who's not annoying you?"

"Cassidy."

"I like him," Charlie said, and his single nod had the gravitas of a gavel strike.

River slumped against the wall in relief.

"Like who?" Bram asked, joining the huddle.

"Cassidy," Charlie said.

"He seems great. I can't wait to ask what kind of tools he uses in his work. Especially to cut bone."

"I heard 'cut bone' and was instantly more interested in this conversation," Wes said, nodding to everyone. "What bone are we cutting?"

"Animal bone," Bram explained.

"Bone is high in phosphorous," said Wes. "Aids in dinoflagellate growth, which—"

"Creates bioluminescence!" everyone chorused.

"Do I really talk about it that much?" Wes muttered.

"Yes," Zachary said. "As you should. It is your passion." He turned to River. "Thank you for bringing me Cassidy. I have an appointment to visit his workshop. I'm quite interested."

River grinned. "You're welcome. I did it just for you."

They left the party to a chorus of well wishes, snow squeaking crisp beneath their shoes.

"I love the smell of this kind of snow," River said, climbing into Cassidy's truck.

Cassidy grinned. "Me too. Reminds me of sledding as a kid and wiping out with my face in the snow."

They drove slowly through the dark streets of Garnet Run. It was late and empty and the snow threw a muffler over the world.

Cassidy slid his hand onto River's thigh and squeezed gently.

"This okay?" he asked.

"It's great. Did you have an okay time? I know it's weird to meet a bunch of people you don't know."

"No, it was wonderful. I love your friends. Thank you for introducing me to them. Zachary's coming to my workshop. I can't wait to ask him about ..."

And Cassidy was off, chatting about the conversations he'd had with each of River's friends.

"I'm so glad you liked them."

"If they're important to you then they're important to me. And I liked them all."

"Gah, I don't want this night to end," River said.

"It doesn't have to. I could come back to your place. If you want?"

River's heart soared.

CHAPTER 24

Cassidy

"I have a present for you that's immediately returnable if you don't like it," River said as they walked through the doors of The Dirt Road Cat Shelter. "And it's imperative that you are honest about if you're not into it. Promise?"

Cassidy smiled to himself.

"Cross my heart and hope to die," he said solemnly.

There was pretty much nothing that River could've gotten him that he wouldn't like because it came from them.

"Okay, cool. I wasn't sure about the whole gift thing because we just ... ya know."

Cassidy nodded.

"We just began," he said.

"Right. Okay, stay here and I'll be right back."

River went into the cat room and Cassidy texted Bram, a conversation with whom had given him the idea for his gift to River.

We all good for later? I'll keep River away from the windows.

All good, Bram replied. *Play music loud and I'll text when I'm done.*

Thank you so much—they'll love it.

"Okay," River said.

They held out a cat carrier. It was Inspector Gadget! Her carrier had a red and green bow tied around it and there was a matching ribbon around her neck that she was attempting to hunt.

"So, I thought that since you and the Inspector here got along so great, you might want her. And before you say yes or no, just know that she can stay here for as long or any time you want. Or if you want her to live here, she totally can."

They ran out of steam and Cassidy's heart was full.

He took the carrier and Inspector Gadget licked at the bars trying to get to him. She was the sweetest thing.

"So you are giving me a cat for Christmas that's also kind of giving yourself a cat?"

River grinned.

"Yes."

They were just beginning this relationship, just learning each other, but Cassidy's first thought in response to River's gift was that it didn't matter if Inspector Gadget came to live with him or stayed here with River, since sooner or later they'd be living together anyway.

Whoa, you're moving way too fast! his logical mind said. But his heart beat to the rhythm of River.

"Thank you, sweetheart. I love her."

He stroked her back with a finger stuck through the opening. She meowed, long and excited.

"I'm so glad. Do you want to take her home, or ..."

Cassidy looked at River's expression intently. He remembered their sadness at succeeding to get cats adopted at Craftmas. They'd miss her if he took her home.

"As much as I'd love to have her at my house because it'd entice you to come over, I think she'd miss all the other cats, being by herself. So maybe she should stay here and be with her friends."

River nodded solemnly but Cassidy saw how their shoulders relaxed.

"Come here," Cassidy said, and pulled River to him in a hug that included the cat carrier.

Inspector Gadget purred loudly.

"You like that, baby?" River cooed to Inspector Gadget. "Okay, we can let her out again if you're not taking her."

Cassidy caught River's chin and kissed them.

"Thank you."

"You're very welcome."

Cassidy slid the arm not holding the cat around River's waist.

"Your gift will be waiting for you when you wake up in the morning," Cassidy said. "I'd love to be here when you get it."

"Why, Mr. Darling," River asked, hand over their mouth, expression one of mock scandalization. "Are you asking to spend the night?

"I am. Any interest in a little *Secaucus Psychic* to wind down?"

River nodded and led Cassidy and Inspector Gadget into the cat room. Cassidy set the carrier on the ground, but before he could even open the latch, he was surrounded by a mewing, purring mob of cats, welcoming Inspector Gadget back as if she'd been gone for months rather than minutes. They rubbed their faces up against the bars and tried to lick her.

"Guess I made the right choice as far as the cat vote is concerned," Cassidy said, flipping the latch and getting out of the line of fire.

The second the door was open, Inspector Gadget was buried under a pile of purrs.

"Guess so," River said. They'd been half acting like whatever Cassidy chose would be fine, but now they let it drop and when they turned to him, their grin was bright enough to light up the room. "I'm so glad she's gonna stay here!"

Cassidy's heart chose that moment to consider River indispensable.

Cassidy wanted them to be happy, to be fulfilled, to be loved. And he wanted to be the one to help all their dreams come true.

He wanted River to come see his workshop and hang out in

the kitchen while Cassidy cooked for them. To come to double feature night with him and Nora on Thursday nights, when they watched a movie that had been considered canonically great and another that was considered terrible and figured out how they were in conversation.

He wanted to wake up with River, who was adorably mumbly and confused after they arose and did adorable, endearing things like drop their forehead to Cassidy's shoulder and groan.

He wanted to sit behind River and play with their hair; pick fluffs of cat fur off their clothes; kiss the spots above their eyebrows that wrinkled when they frowned.

He wanted to attend more events with River's gang of friends and be included in their referential patter. He wanted secrets with River and dreams and private jokes.

He wanted to make River feel loved and cared for and supported and he wanted it now. Even though it was early, Cassidy could see his love for River floating over the next rise on the horizon, inevitable, if the course remained clear.

"So," River said. "*Secaucus Psychic?*"

Cassidy wanted to watch TV with them, to cuddle with them, to chat about the show and fall asleep together.

"Yes. Absolutely."

And they watched, snuggling on the cushions, until River fell asleep against Cassidy's shoulder.

Done, came the text from Bram. *Have a great Christmas.*

Thank you so much. I owe you one.

It was late and River woke when Cassidy turned off the television.

"You wanna go to bed, sweetheart?" Cassidy asked.

"Mhm."

River was halfway asleep anyway, and they trudged upstairs slowly and fell right into bed.

Cassidy curled himself around River and they snuggled back into him, pulling his arm across their chest.

"Hi," they murmured, kissing his hand.

"Hi," Cassidy responded, heart a puddle.

"Okay, night," River mumbled.

"Good night, baby."

River's soft *hmmmm* told Cassidy they liked that, and Cassidy spent the minutes before he fell asleep trying to catalogue all the things he wanted to do with River, the places he wanted them to go together, the meals he wanted to cook for them.

He thought of River's vision board and how what they wanted more than anything was a place of their own. Space to run their life on their own terms. It was what Cassidy wanted also—what he already had in the works. It soothed him more than he wanted to admit that they were compatible in their goals for the future.

CHAPTER 25

River

River woke, as they so often did, to a cat tail flicking their nose. They reached out a hand to pet whichever beast was there and gently encourage them away from their face. It was Inspector Gadget.

"Go stalk your new daddy," River grumbled. Then they scooped up the cat and placed her on Cassidy's chest, which rose and fell peacefully with his slumbering breaths.

Inspector Gadget nestled into Cassidy's armpit without waking him and River fell back asleep.

The next time they awoke it was a slow drift back into consciousness from a warm caress up and down their side. They nestled backward into to Cassidy and felt the twitch of his erection against their ass.

Cassidy hummed and gathered them closer, placing soft kisses on their shoulder, neck, hair.

"Morning."

"Don't stop," River murmured.

They were luxuriating in the land between slumber and waking, when their consciousness hadn't yet kicked in enough to make them feel awkward.

Cassidy's hand danced along their ribs. His hands were always warm, no matter how cold it was outside, and sometimes when he saw River was cold, he'd slide a hand under their shirt, pressing heat into their skin.

His fingertips were rough on the tender skin of their nipples and when he pinched them a little, River writhed, electricity shooting straight to their crotch. Then Cassidy's hand was there too, working them with a dreamy pressure.

River thrust backward, grinding into Cassidy's hard cock. Cassidy shuddered and moaned and then River was completely surrounded, the space between their bodies gone, their breath hot.

"You're so fucking hot," Cassidy murmured and River turned in his arms to catch his mouth in a kiss.

They kissed deeply and ground together.

The bolt of pleasure that shot through River nearly made them dizzy and they climbed on top of Cassidy. He loved when they did this. His eyes always went hooded and lustful and this time was no exception.

River leaned down for a kiss and Cassidy's arms encircled their back. When the kiss ended, River pressed their bodies together from chest to thigh, shuddering as waves of pleasure pulsed through them.

The began a slow and dirty grind together that quickly turned desperate. River's blood felt fizzy, their muscles liquid.

"Fuck, baby, c'mere."

Cassidy's big hands splayed across River's hips and ass as he dragged River onto his lap. River's hips and spine were loose and their thighs were tight as they rocked. Cassidy took their whole weight easily, leaving River to seek their pleasure however they wished.

They braced on his chest and ground on Cassidy Darling like he was a sex toy. Which, from the volume of his exclamations and the lust in his eyes, was working great for Cassidy as well.

When they fucked like this, it made River feel liquid, like their body flowed into Cassidy's. Their pleasure was honey thick and slow, and they never wanted it to end. But too soon, their body reached the top of its climb and tumbled down into a clenching, muscular orgasm that wrung them out until all they could do was cling to Cassidy as he roared out his own pleasure.

Cassidy's tenderness after sex was disarming and left River feeling shy and trembly in the best ways. This morning, though, he seemed to gaze deeper into River's eyes; his kisses were softer; his hands more seeking.

"Thanks for taking me to the party with you," he said, eyes bright. "I liked meeting your friends."

River stretched luxuriantly, so sated and comfortable that, left to their own devices, they'd fall right back asleep.

"I'm glad you came," they said into Cassidy's soft, comfy chest. "They all loved you."

Their pillow disappeared.

"Wait, what, they did? Did they tell you that? What did they say? Who said it?"

River said an internal goodbye to the three more hours of sleep they'd have preferred and dragged themself up.

"Yes, they all told me. They think you're great."

Cassidy was practically vibrating in place, so River took pity on him and repeated everything everyone had said to the best of their memory. Cassidy smiled, relaxing again.

"Thank god. I can't believe you didn't tell me that last night!"

"Gotta keep you on your toes," River said.

But the truth was that it had never occurred to them that things would go any other way, and they'd assumed it had been clear how much everyone adored him.

"So, can I show you your Christmas present now?" Cassidy asked excitedly.

"Sure."

River teetered out of bed, awaiting further instructions.

"Okay." Cassidy guided them to the bedroom window and stood behind them. His bare chest was warm at their back and he smelled like sex.

He pulled the curtains aside and River blinked at the sudden brightness of the snow. As their eyes adjusted, though, they began to see something strange.

"What am I looking at?" they asked, but before Cassidy could answer, their brain and eyes agreed that they were seeing huge, green— "Cats!"

The tops of the evergreen bushes and trees around the shelter had been shaped into rounded cat heads and bodies with pointed ears on top. They were of all sizes and shapes, depending on the evergreen, but together they formed a feline army, standing in protection of the shelter and everyone inside it.

It was like a dream or a video game come to life and River couldn't look away.

"Holy shit, how?"

"Bram did it. Do you like?"

River felt like they had fallen asleep some weeks ago in the real world—a world that had not, historically, been terribly kind to them—and woken up in a fantasy where things were soft and warm and comfortable; where there were kisses and hugs and pleasure and care and, well, huge evergreen cats. It was magic that could all be traced back to the arrival of Cassidy Darling in their life.

"They're in front of the windows downstairs too, so you can see them from the front desk," Cassidy murmured into their neck.

River pulled on clothes and raced down the stairs to stand before the huge windows. From the ground level, their size was even more impressive. One cat had a paw raised, like it was waving to them, or about to swipe at the building. A row of bushes formed the body of a sleeping cat. And all around the parking lot were cats of different sizes and shapes.

"Damn," Cassidy said, "Bram did an amazing job."

River turned to thank Cassidy, then suddenly there were tears streaming down their face.

"What's wrong, baby?" Cassidy asked.

"This is the sweetest thing anyone has ever done for me," they said. "When Rye gave me this job and this apartment, that was the most generous and amazing moment of my life. Cuz I didn't think I could ever ... But this is ..."

They dissolved into tears.

"I wanted you to be able to look out any window in your home and work and see something that might make you smile," Cassidy said, stroking their hair as they cried. "I love your smile."

Once, their friend Tracey had told River that they had a first level smile that was for everyone and a second level smile that was only for friends. River thought they might have reached a third level of smile they'd never known they were capable of: a natural, automatic smile that they didn't try and control. It hadn't come out before Cassidy, but they could feel it now.

It felt like a flame kindled in their heart that leaked into their face. It felt like joy and hope and trust. It felt like the kind of smile that grew out of a substrate so strong it could support the heavy fruit of big feelings.

"Cassidy," River tried.

Their voice was rough and tears still welled in their eyes. They didn't know how to thank him in a way that felt commensurate with their feelings.

"River," Cassidy replied, as if that had been a full sentence. "I'm totally falling for you in case you can't tell."

Me too! screamed the voice inside River that wanted to meet Cassidy halfway in everything. But *Scary, scary, scary* was there too.

"I'm ... I can tell," is what came out of their mouth.

Cassidy looked surprised, then laughed.

"Well, I guess I'm not one to hide my feelings."

"I am," River admitted.

Cassidy nodded thoughtfully.

"If, hypothetically, you *weren't* hiding your feelings, what might they say?" he asked.

River stepped into Cassidy, whose arms instantly enfolded them. They rested their head on Cassidy's shoulder and breathed him in.

"I'd say, me too," River said softly into the cotton of Cassidy's T-shirt.

Cassidy's heart sped beneath their hand.

"I'm pretty enthusiastic about that," Cassidy said.

"I'm pretty enthusiastic about it too," River said.

Their stomach growled.

"Do you know how to make pancakes?"

"Mhm," Cassidy said.

Of course he did.

"If you make me pancakes, I'll love you forever," River teased.

Cassidy sprinted to the kitchen, leaving River laughing. They followed to find Cassidy already flipping through the cabinets.

"You don't have any butter, syrup, or baking soda," he said, at a loss. "Is this a weird challenge, like make pancakes out of cat food or something? Because while I really, *really* want your undying love, I assure you, I don't think I'm up to the task. Neither's my gag reflex."

"Oh, right."

Cassidy laughed.

"Why don't you let me take you out for pancakes at Peach's Diner?" he offered. "Have you been there?"

"Once or twice." River grinned. "That sounds perfect."

"Okay, good, because I have a lot of questions about this whole you falling for me thing."

River felt their cheeks heat.

"Yeah, I could maybe be convinced to answer some of those questions for you," they said. "If you can make it through the gauntlet of cats that stand between us and your truck."

"I would go through any gauntlet to get you pancakes," Cassidy proclaimed bravely. "Shall we?"

He tossed the spatula on the counter and held his elbow out, all chivalry.

"Hold on, I have to feed like a million cats first."

Cassidy brushed his thumb over River's cheekbone and River leaned into the contact.

"Well then, that's the gauntlet I will go through," he pledged. "Show me where the cat food is? The faster we do this, the faster we get pancakes."

They fed the cats together, and River let themself imagine what it might be like not to be alone.

They were standing where River had first seen Cassidy. How could that have been only a month ago? How could everything have changed this quickly?

But things changed when they changed, River knew, and only a fool said no to the chance for a life they had dreamed of.

"You with me?" Cassidy asked.

River couldn't know what the future would hold, couldn't know what barriers or problems they might face. But what they did know was that Cassidy Darling was standing in their foyer slash cat shelter front desk area, waiting to whisk River away for pancakes, and offering to be a continued part of their life.

And that was all they needed to know to say, "Yes."

THE END ...
Now check out the rest of the Garnet Run series!

Thank you so much for reading **Shelter in Garnet Run**! I hope you enjoyed River and Cassidy's story. If you did, check out the rest of the Garnet Run series!

There are several easter eggs from other books too:

Did the name Mikal sound familiar to you? It's an easter egg you might recognize from *Out of Nowhere (Middle of Somewhere #2)*.

Did you hear beeswax and think of *The Holiday Trap*? That's an easter egg too!

The band Riven is from *Riven*, my reluctant rock star series, as is the fictional show, *Secaucus Psychic*.

It's all connected, so read on and discover more crossovers!

xo, Roan Parrish

Want to get exclusive content, news of future book releases, and a FREE HOLIDAY ROMANCE? Sign up for my **NEWSLETTER**!

Also by Roan Parrish

The Better Than People Series

Better Than People

Best Laid Plans

The Pride of Garnet Run (free novella)

The Lights on Knockbridge Lane

The Rivals of Casper Road

The Middle of Somewhere Series

In the Middle of Somewhere

Out of Nowhere

Where We Left Off

The Small Change Series:

Small Change

Invitation to the Blues

A Good, Old-Fashioned Chanukah Pegging (free short)

The Riven Series

Riven

Rend

Raze

Standalones

The Remaking of Corbin Wale

Natural Enemies

Heart of the Steal

Thrall

The Holiday Trap

About the Author

Roan Parrish lives in upstate New York, where she is gradually attempting to write love stories in every genre.

When not writing, she can usually be found cutting her friends' hair, meandering through whatever city she's in while listening to torch songs and melodic death metal, or cooking overly elaborate meals. She loves bonfires, winter beaches, minor chord harmonies, and self-tattooing. One time she may or may not have baked a six-layer chocolate cake and then thrown it out the window in a fit of pique.

You can keep up with all of Roan's new releases and get exclusive free content by signing up for her newsletter at roanparrish.com. And you can find her online at RoanParrish in all the usual places.

www.ingramcontent.com/pod-product-compliance
Lightning Source LLC
Chambersburg PA
CBHW070508200726
48293CB00007B/2444